A MYSTERY IN BLOOM:

RUIN IN THE ROSES

(An Alice Bloom Cozy Mystery—Book Two)

FIONA GRACE

Fiona Grace

Fiona Grace is author of the LACEY DOYLE COZY MYSTERY series, comprising nine books; of the TUSCAN VINEYARD COZY MYSTERY series, comprising seven books; of the DUBIOUS WITCH COZY MYSTERY series, comprising three books; of the BEACHFRONT BAKERY COZY MYSTERY series, comprising six books; of the CATS AND DOGS COZY MYSTERY series, comprising nine books; of the ELIZA MONTAGU COZY MYSTERY series, comprising nine books (and counting); of the ENDLESS HARBOR ROMANTIC COMEDY series, comprising nine books (and counting); of the INN AT DUNE ISLAND ROMANTIC COMEDY series, comprising five books (and counting); of the INN BY THE SEA ROMANTIC COMEDY series, comprising five books (and counting); of the MAID AND THE MANSION COZY MYSTERY series, comprising five books (and counting); of the ALICE BLOOM COZY MYSTERY series, comprising five books (and counting); and of the TIMBERLAKE TITANS HOCKEY ROMANCE series, comprising five books (and counting).

Fiona would love to hear from you, so please visit www.fionagraceauthor.com to receive free ebooks, hear the latest news, and stay in touch.

ISBN: 978-1-0943-9799-3

BOOKS BY FIONA GRACE

TIMBERLAKE TITANS HOCKEY ROMANCE
RINKSIDE ROMANCE (Book #1)
FLIRTY FACEOFF (Book #2)
MELTING THE ICE (Book #3)
THE PUCK STOPS HERE (Book #4)
GLOVES DROP, LOVE BLOOMS (Book #5)

THE MAID AND THE MANSION COZY MYSTERY
A MYSTERIOUS MURDER (Book #1)
A SCANDALOUS DEATH (Book #2)
A MISSING GUEST (Book #3)
AN UNSOLVABLE CRIME (Book #4)
AN IMPOSSIBLE HEIST (Book #5)

INN BY THE SEA ROMANTIC COMEDY
A NEW LOVE (Book #1)
A NEW CHANCE (Book #2)
A NEW HOME (Book #3)
A NEW LIFE (Book #4)
A NEW ME (Book #5)

THE INN AT DUNE ISLAND ROMANTIC COMEDY
A CHANCE LOVE (Book #1)
A CHANCE FALL (Book #2)
A CHANCE ROMANCE (Book #3)
A CHANCE CHRISTMAS (Book #4)
A CHANCE ENGAGEMENT (Book #5)

ENDLESS HARBOR ROMANTIC COMEDY
ALWAYS, WITH YOU (Book #1)
ALWAYS, FOREVER (Book #2)
ALWAYS, PLUS ONE (Book #3)
ALWAYS, TOGETHER (Book #4)
ALWAYS, LIKE THIS (Book #5)
ALWAYS, FATED (Book #6)

ALWAYS, FOR LOVE (Book #7)
ALWAYS, JUST US (Book #8)
ALWAYS, IN LOVE (Book #9)

ELIZA MONTAGU COZY MYSTERY
MURDER AT THE HEDGEROW (Book #1)
A DALLOP OF DEATH (Book #2)
CALAMITY AT THE BALL (Book #3)
A SPEAKEASY DEMISE (Book #4)
A FLAPPER FATALITY (Book #5)
BUMPED BY A DAME (Book #6)
A DOLL'S DEBACLE (Book #7)
A FELLA'S RUIN (Book #8)
A GAL'S OFFING (Book #9)

LACEY DOYLE COZY MYSTERY
MURDER IN THE MANOR (Book#1)
DEATH AND A DOG (Book #2)
CRIME IN THE CAFE (Book #3)
VEXED ON A VISIT (Book #4)
KILLED WITH A KISS (Book #5)
PERISHED BY A PAINTING (Book #6)
SILENCED BY A SPELL (Book #7)
FRAMED BY A FORGERY (Book #8)
CATASTROPHE IN A CLOISTER (Book #9)

TUSCAN VINEYARD COZY MYSTERY
AGED FOR MURDER (Book #1)
AGED FOR DEATH (Book #2)
AGED FOR MAYHEM (Book #3)
AGED FOR SEDUCTION (Book #4)
AGED FOR VENGEANCE (Book #5)
AGED FOR ACRIMONY (Book #6)
AGED FOR MALICE (Book #7)

DUBIOUS WITCH COZY MYSTERY
SKEPTIC IN SALEM: AN EPISODE OF MURDER (Book #1)
SKEPTIC IN SALEM: AN EPISODE OF CRIME (Book #2)
SKEPTIC IN SALEM: AN EPISODE OF DEATH (Book #3)

BEACHFRONT BAKERY COZY MYSTERY

BEACHFRONT BAKERY: A KILLER CUPCAKE (Book #1)
BEACHFRONT BAKERY: A MURDEROUS MACARON (Book #2)
BEACHFRONT BAKERY: A PERILOUS CAKE POP (Book #3)
BEACHFRONT BAKERY: A DEADLY DANISH (Book #4)
BEACHFRONT BAKERY: A TREACHEROUS TART (Book #5)
BEACHFRONT BAKERY: A CALAMITOUS COOKIE (Book #6)

CATS AND DOGS COZY MYSTERY
A VILLA IN SICILY: OLIVE OIL AND MURDER (Book #1)
A VILLA IN SICILY: FIGS AND A CADAVER (Book #2)
A VILLA IN SICILY: VINO AND DEATH (Book #3)
A VILLA IN SICILY: CAPERS AND CALAMITY (Book #4)
A VILLA IN SICILY: ORANGE GROVES AND VENGEANCE
(Book #5)
A VILLA IN SICILY: CANNOLI AND A CASUALTY (Book #6)

ALICE BLOOM COZY MYSTERY
MURDER IN THE MARIGOLDS (Book #1)
RUIN IN THE ROSES (Book #2)
DECEIT IN THE DAFFODILS (Book #3)
SCANDAL IN THE SAFFRON (Book #4)
CATASTROPHE IN THE CARNATIONS (Book #5)

PROLOGUE

Alice Bloom pushed open the door to the Steeping Leaf, a tea shop nestled in the heart of Hampton. The bell above the door tinkled, announcing her arrival. The aroma of steeping herbs and fragrant blooms greeted her. She smiled. Jazz Patel, her best friend since second grade, had created a shop that was as warm and comforting as she was herself. The faint sunlight of early spring in New England filtered through the windows, casting warm patterns on the wooden floors.

"Ah, the prodigal plant whisperer returns!" Jazz called out from behind the counter, her eyes twinkling above the steam rising from a freshly poured cup of tea.

"Only because I know where to find the best chamomile blend in town," Alice replied with a smile of her own as she approached the counter.

Jazz handed her a cup adorned with delicate floral patterns. "I brewed this one just for you – hints of lavender and lemon balm. It's calming, with a touch of zest, much like yourself."

"You're too kind in so many ways." It was nice to feel appreciated. Alice inhaled deeply, the scent grounding her after weeks of adapting back to her hometown's slower rhythm following a whirlwind trip to the Italian Riviera. She settled onto one of the stools at the counter where she could watch Jazz work and enjoy her tea at the same time. "Tell me everything."

"Have you seen Old Man Henderson's place lately?" Jazz asked, leaning on the counter across from Alice.

"Only from the street. I'm not sure I've ever seen red cedar grow that dense and that high," Alice mused. "Any more theories on what he's hiding back there?"

"Rumor has it he's hiding a treasure trove of rare orchids, or a legendary heirloom rose," Jazz said, eyebrows raised.

It had better not be the orchids. The last thing Alice needed was her ex — Scott Thorne orchid hunter — to invade her hometown and he definitely would if there were rare orchids around.

"Or maybe a less romantic compost pile gone rogue," Alice laughed, but the mystery of Henderson's hidden garden itched at her like a seed waiting to sprout and had since she was a teenager. "Someday we're going to have to sneak in there and find out."

"Wouldn't it be something if he had a garden that rivaled the botanical wonders of the world? Imagine stumbling upon a tucked-away Eden right here in Hampton," Jazz continued.

"Eden or not, I wish I could take a peek. I could help. I'm sure I could add something to whatever effort he has going on back there." Alice hoped the way she approached landscaping projects with a blend of scientific knowledge and aesthetics meant she would almost always have a suggestion that could be helpful.

"Maybe you should offer your services. A little neighborly landscaping advice could go a long way," Jazz suggested with a sly grin. "Then you could snoop along the way."

"Oh, sure," Alice replied. "Something tells me Old Man Henderson isn't looking for a consult. He acts all grumpy, but I think he likes a topic of conversation around town, making people guess at his secret."

"I can see that. But secrets have a way of surfacing, especially in Hampton. What if he has something really damning buried back there?" Jazz waggled her eyebrows and sang, "Dun-dun-duuuun."

"Let's hope Old Man Henderson's secret are the kind that don't require too much digging," Alice said, taking another sip of her tea and giving a contented sigh. "I'd like to keep my hometown murder-free." She'd had more than enough of murder on her trip to Italy.

Alice traced the rim of her porcelain teacup, feeling the warmth radiate through the delicate china and create some contentment in her soul. Spending time with Jazz in her tea shop helped a lot. She'd taken on a few small projects close to the area since returning from Italy, but nothing that required travel. It had been good to have a break and to have some time to recharge and reconnect.

"Speaking of secrets," Jazz asked, "how's the Chef Hottie McHotToque?"

"Ah, Marco Bellamy," Alice said, feeling the faint blush creep up her cheeks. They'd met in Italy and bonded over their love of plants and good food and how that all could come together. She could almost smell the fragrant blend of herbs that seemed to cling to him wherever he went. Her hand went to her mouth remembering what his kisses had been like. She sighed. "We've been exchanging emails. He's pretty busy these days."

"Any chance he'll be crossing paths with Hampton's most talented landscape designer again?" Jazz prodded, leaning forward.

"Unlikely," Alice replied, shaking her head. "He's in California right now, working on a project involving edible flowers. The man has a knack for blending taste and aesthetics. Quite a few of the high-end restaurants in wine country have asked him to consult on ways to elevate their dishes."

"Sounds like he knows his way around a bouquet, both in a vase and on a plate. A shame he's so far away," Jazz sighed, pouring more tea into Alice's cup. "But who knows what the future holds, right?"

"Right," Alice echoed, though her tone held a hint of resignation. Her life, much like Marco's, was a series of commissions, taking her from one place to another, often without a lot of notice. She loved the work, but each new job pulled her further from the establishing roots of her own.

Before she could dwell on the thought, the cheerful ring of her cell phone cut through the calm ambiance of the tea shop. Alice excused herself and fished the device from her handbag, checking the caller ID before answering.

"Owen Fieldstone," she announced to Jazz before ducking out of the tea shop and pressing the phone to her ear. "This should be interesting."

"Bloom," Owen's gruff voice came through the speaker, tinged with a rare note of excitement. "I hope you're ready for that trip to France. The job we bid on—the cottage garden for that winery in Provence—it's ours."

Alice's heart skipped a beat as she processed the news. "Really? That's incredible! When do they want to start?" She bounced on her toes like a runner ready to start a race.

"Immediately," Owen confirmed. "They're eager to have the design in place before the summer tourists descend upon them and something about a competition. I told them we have the best designer for the job, and they agreed without hesitation."

"Provence," Alice whispered, her mind already envisioning rows of lavender and rustic stone pathways. "A cottage garden amidst the vineyards..." Oh, this was going to be fun.

"Pack your bags, Bloom," Owen continued, bringing her back to reality. "You're our star, and this is your stage. Make us proud."

"Thank you, Owen. I'll do my best," she promised, her professional demeanor slipping back into place.

"You always do, Alice." There was a grudgingly proud note to his voice that had Alice ducking her head at the praise. "Do me a favor, though. Try to stay out of trouble?"

She laughed. "I'll do my best at that, too." It wasn't like she sought trouble out. It just seemed to find her.

As she ended the call, Alice felt a surge of anticipation. Designing a garden in Provence was a dream many in her field coveted. This was more than just another project; it was a canvas where her expertise and creativity could flourish.

Alice ended the call and walked back into the tea shop, grateful for its warmth.

"And?" Jazz prompted. "What's the new job? Where are you going next?"

With a giggle, Alice said, "Provence!" And then did a little happy dance.

Jazz was practically vibrating with excitement. "Provence? You're going to design in Provence, Alice!" Jazz's brown eyes sparkled like the topaz pendants she often wore around her neck.

"Looks like it," Alice replied, her voice a mix of pride and awe. A cottage garden in France was the sort of job that could define a career. She couldn't help but beam at the thought.

"Before you even start packing for France, you have to call Daisy," Jazz insisted, reaching for a scone from the tiered stand between them. "She'll have just the right eco-chic outfits for those Provencal fields. Imagine the photos!"

Alice chuckled, knowing her sister's penchant for blending style with sustainability and making sure all of it ended up on social media. "She'll be thrilled... right after she gives me the 'be careful' lecture."

"Can you blame her? After your Italian adventure, we all want to wrap you in bubble wrap." Jazz rolled her eyes, taking a sip of her tea.

"None of that was my doing. I'm just a landscape designer who happened to be at the wrong place at the wrong time," Alice said, feigning innocence.

"Which brings me to my next point," Jazz said, setting down her cup with a determined clatter. "Promise me you'll stick to the garden paths this time. No sleuthing in Provence, okay? We don't want you getting kidnapped by rogue vintners or something."

"Jazz, I'm flattered that you think my life is as exciting as a spy novel, but really, what are the odds of that happening again?" Alice leaned back in her chair. "Italy was a one-time thing. Provence will be all about the wisteria and wine, nothing more."

"Good," Jazz nodded approvingly. "Because if you're not careful, I'll tell Daisy to pack you a Kevlar vest instead of a sundress."

"Ha! As if she'd ever sacrifice fashion for function," Alice said. But inwardly, she resolved to heed Jazz's advice. Italy had been a lesson in unexpected dangers, and she wouldn't soon forget it. Provence would be different — what to plant in its serene landscapes was the only mystery she planned to unravel.

CHAPTER ONE

Alice's eyes fluttered open as the car rolled to a gentle stop.

"We are here, mademoiselle," the driver, Jean-Baptiste, said. He got out and walked over to her side of the vehicle to open her door.

He had dark hair that had that effortlessly tousled look that Alice was pretty sure took a fair amount of time in front of a mirror. Tall and thin, he wore a slim-fitting button-down shirt over neatly pressed jeans. A scarf looped loosely around his neck that somehow didn't look affected at all. Instead, along with his high cheekbones, it gave him a certain French flair.

She stepped out of the car, her legs thankful for the solid ground. The journey had been long, the hum of the plane's engines now replaced by the chirping of birds and the rustle of olive branches in the breeze. She gazed up at the Château DuPont. It stood proudly before her, its silhouette a testament to centuries past, nestled in the embrace of Provence's sun-drenched hills.

"I will see that your bag gets to your room," Jean-Baptiste said.

"Thank you so much, Jean-Baptiste. I'm sorry I wasn't better company on the drive." Alice hoped she hadn't drooled too much while she'd napped.

"Not at all." He gave her a small salute and removed her bag from the trunk and walked toward the château.

The château itself beckoned with an air of timeless elegance, its history etched into every stone block. Alice ran a hand through her hair, brushing away the weariness of travel. She had come at René Dupont's behest, the master vintner whose proposals spoke of a need for renewal in his gardens—a challenge to which her green thumb itched to rise. The estate sprawled before her, vineyards unfurling like green ribbons amidst the rolling landscape, olive groves standing sentinel across the terrain. In the distance, a mountain peak rose. She felt like she'd wandered into a painting by Cézanne.

Her gaze wandered to the formal gardens. They were a patchwork of color—some bedraggled hydrangeas in hues of blue and purple, calla lilies, roses that climbed trellises with thorny grace and hedges of yew. The warm, golden light brought out the vivid colors of the landscape, from the rich greens of the vineyards and olive groves to the vibrant purple hues of the lavender fields in the distance. The grounds were pretty, but a little old-fashioned and stuffy, everything carefully symmetrical and geometric. DuPont had spoken of wanting a cottage garden. Something that felt less formal and melded more with the beauty of nature that surrounded the estate and the relaxed nature of Provencal living.

The potential she saw here stirred something within Alice. She could already envision creating more meandering pathways that could be punctuated by hidden nooks and botanical surprises. She took a few steps onto the driveway, her gaze drawn upward to the majestic Château DuPont. Its façade blazed with the earthy warmth of ochre, the pigment sourced from the very soil upon which it stood, painting a picture of harmonious elegance against the Provencal sky. The grand entrance beckoned with an air of welcome, and the turrets reached for the heavens, their silhouettes etching an idyllic scene from a bygone era. "Wow," she said under her breath.

"Mademoiselle Bloom!" A voice rich with a French accent cut through the air. René Dupont emerged from the shadow of the entrance, his presence seemed intertwined with the château itself—dignified, rooted, yet brimming with charm. His hair, a distinguished silver, framed his face, and his eyes sparkled with the vivacity of youth despite the lines that time and exposure to the sun had etched around them.

"Please, call me Alice." Alice replied as she accepted the outstretched hand. His grip was firm and his smile welcoming.

"Monsieur Fieldstone told me that you would make my gardens beautiful. He didn't mention how beautiful you were yourself. Your hair, it is like a beautiful sunset and your skin is like porcelain."

Hoo, boy. Here came another blush.

"Allow me to introduce my assistant, Sophie Moreau," René said, gesturing to a woman who appeared at his side immediately.

"It is a pleasure, Mademoiselle. If there's anything you need, please do not hesitate to ask." She had long brown hair pie,rcing blue eyes, and an air of confidence and sophistication. Although her clothes were clearly chosen for working outside, she wore them as if they were the latest fashion trend.

Ah, the French. They really were a wonder. Alice hoped she could make the garden live up to them. "Thank you, Sophie. It's lovely to meet you," Alice responded.

Before Sophie could say anything more, René interrupted. "Sophie, please go to the barrel room and see if we need to top anything off."

Sophie frowned. "But René, the rosé is in the steel—"

René cut her off again, his tone harsh. "I said to check the barrels."

Sophie pressed her lips together in a tight line and gave her boss a slight nod of the head and gave Alice a warm smile as she hurried off along the side of the château.

"Come, let us go inside," René said, leading Alice across the threshold. "You see, Sophie must see if the barrels are full. It's very important to fill the spaces caused by evaporation in the barrels. We don't want the wine having too much air contact."

"I'll take your word for that," Alice said, following him into the château. "I don't know a lot about making wine. Although I do like to drink it."

"We'll make sure you get to do more than a little of that!" René said with a smile. "We nearly brush our teeth with it here."

The interior of the château unfolded like a living tapestry, each corner a testament to the opulence that only centuries of care could cultivate. Antique furnishings adorned every room, their wood gleaming with a patina that spoke of endless polishings and careful restorations. Tapestries hung from the walls, intricate threads weaving stories of valor and romance, while ornate chandeliers cast a golden glow upon the scenes below.

"Please, make yourself comfortable," René offered, gesturing to a plush sofa as he settled into the armchair opposite.

Almost on cue, a Black woman wearing a black blouse and trousers under a bistro apron arrived bearing a silver tray. With quiet efficiency, she set down two flutes of sparkling champagne , followed by a plate of warm gougères that released a tempting aroma of cheese into the air.

"Ah, thank you, Lilou. Nothing quite says 'welcome' like a good glass of bubbly and some local delicacies," René remarked with an appreciative glance at the housekeeper, who nodded and retreated with the same silent grace. He raised his glass. "To our new endeavor."

"Thank you, this is wonderful," Alice said, taking a sip of the champagne. The effervescence danced on her tongue, a lively prelude to the savory richness of the gougères she tasted next. In this moment, surrounded by the embrace of history and the promise of creative fulfillment, Alice felt a sense of belonging blossoming within her. She was exactly where she needed to be, and the adventure was just beginning. It was enough to combat the jet lag that had had her napping in the car on the way down. "How long has your family lived here?"

"My family? The DuPonts have been making wine here since the mid-1500s." He smiled and glanced over at a set of portraits that graced the walls of the salon. "Provence was France's first wine-making region."

Alice looked over at the portraits, then stood to get a closer look at one in particular. It was of a woman with beautiful smooth skin, touched by color on each cheek, her hair piled on her head. What drew Alice, though, was the background. She emerged from a cloud of roses of different colors. "Is this one of your ancestors?"

"Indeed. You have a good eye. That is my mother. Jeannete DuPont. She was a woman of great beauty and grace and also quite a talented vintner," DuPont said with clear pride in his voice. He set down his champagne flute on a mahogany side table with a soft clink, his gaze wandering through the nearby French doors that opened to the château's gardens. The late afternoon sun bathed the grounds in a golden hue, casting long shadows among the hydrangeas and roses.

"Charming as these interiors are, I often find myself longing for a place out there," he motioned towards the garden, "where one can sit and truly savor the estate's offerings." His hands gestured expansively, encompassing not just the room but the vision he held for his land.

Alice followed his gaze, her eyes reflecting the same spark of possibility that always ignited when she considered a new project. "I can see it now," she mused aloud, "intimate seating nestled between the blooms, perhaps a pergola draped in wisteria to frame the view."

"Exactly!" René exclaimed, leaning forward. "These kinds of formal gardens don't really fit how we live and entertain anymore. I want something both elegant and casual, something that reflects our commitment to sustainability and Provence's roots, but is still beautiful."

Alice nodded for a second or two as she thought. "Yes. A cottage garden will totally work," she said, finally. "It has its roots in traditions that go back centuries, but reflect modern ideas of how to live with nature and support it."

"Monsieur Owen told me you were perceptive and had a deep knowledge of landscaping through the ages. He clearly was correct. I think we already have the beginning of a plan. Might we add some hydrangeas?" René sat back in his chair and crossed one leg over his knee.

"Hydrangeas?" Alice asked.

"Oui, Mademoiselle Alice. They were my mother's favorite flower and the ones in our garden here haven't been doing well for some reason. This summer will be the tenth anniversary of her passing. I've named one of our new rosés after her and want to present it among her favorites." René looked down at the floor as he spoke.

Alice knew all too well what it was like to lose a parent too soon and allowed René a moment to gather himself. "What a lovely way to honor her. "

"With the rosé competition approaching, I wish to present not merely the finest wine but an experience that celebrates our traditions and encompasses the beauty of Château DuPont—inside and out."

"Rosé competition?" she asked. Owen had mentioned something about a competition, but she didn't have any details.

"Yes, yes." René nodded his head. "In just a few months, Château DuPont will be competing in the Guerre de Rosé. The competition is largely local, but since Provence is known for its rosés, winning confers a great deal of respect. I would love for my mother's rosé to be among the winners." He frowned. "I would also like to make a few of my rivals give me the respect I deserve."

"Anyone in particular?" Alice asked.

"Oui. Too many to mention. Claire LeBlanc and Henri Rousseau have been particular thorns in my side since my mother's passing, but they are not alone. There are others." He shook his head. "Their disrespect has been galling."

"I see." Alice nodded, feeling the weight of expectation mingling with the thrill of creation. She would design a garden that married function with aesthetics, a space where the essence of Provence could be tasted on the tongue and felt in the heart. It had already captured hers.

"Consider it done, Monsieur DuPont," Alice said with a quiet confidence that was new to her. She raised her glass in a toast to the project ahead.

***

Lilou led Alice up a grand staircase, the steps whispering echoes of bygone elegance beneath their feet. At the top landing, they turned down a corridor lined with paintings of landscapes that looked very much like what she'd seen outside at different times of the year, even some with snow although that rarely happened in this part of France.

"Your chamber, Mademoiselle Bloom," the housekeeper said, opening a door to reveal a room awash with the soft light of the setting sun. It spilled through tall windows, illuminating the pristine white linens of a canopied bed.

"Merci, Lilou," Alice replied, stepping into the space that immediately felt like a haven. Her gaze was drawn to the windows, where she could see the expanse of the garden below. From this vantage point, she noted the sporadic coverage of the flowers and the lack of suitable seating that would invite one to linger amidst the fragrance and color. "Please call me Alice."

Already, her mind whirled with ideas of flowering herbs that might line the paths, the strategic placement of benches made from reclaimed wood, and trellises that would encourage climbing roses to reach skyward. She imagined guests pausing to admire a particular bloom or to watch bees dip into the hearts of flowers, all while enjoying a glass of René's prized rosé. Her heart beat a little faster. Part of her wanted to get started immediately. Another part was insisting on a good night's sleep before she really dug in.

As the sun dipped lower, casting a warm glow over the room, Alice unpacked her belongings, each item finding its place within the antique armoire or atop the dresser. With each fold and tuck, she settled more into the role she was here to play—a weaver of natural beauty, a caretaker of living art.

Once settled, she took out her computer and started a video chat with Jazz and Daisy. They both answered within seconds.

"So?" Daisy prompted. "How is it?"

"I don't have words," Alice said. "Let me show you."

She picked up the computer and walked it around so they could see the room and get a glimpse of the gardens outside.

Jazz squealed. "It's like a movie! So gorgeous!"

Alice smiled. "I know. Monsieur DuPont seems very nice, too. I can see already some of what I want to do."

"Of course you can," Daisy said with a grin. "Go get 'em, sister."

"I intend to." They said good-bye and Alice stepped back to the window, resting her hands on the cool stone sill. The gardens beckoned to her, whispered secrets of what they could become under her guidance. She smiled, accepting the challenge and the promise of transformation that lay before her.

CHAPTER TWO

Sunlight streamed through the latticed windows as Alice took a final sip of her café au lait, the richness of the brew complementing the flakiness of the croissant she had just finished. The country French kitchen exuded warmth and charm, but the garden beyond called to her. Pushing back her chair with purpose, Alice stood. "Thank you, Lilou. That was delicious."

Lilou smiled. "You are very easy to please, Mademoiselle Alice." She picked up Alice's cup and plate before Alice had a chance to take them to the sink herself.

Alice laughed. "Not everyone thinks so!" Stepping out into the garden, she put on her straw hat to keep the sun off her fair skin. She had on her usual gardening ensemble of overalls and clogs with a light cardigan over it all to ward off the morning chill. Even though she doubted she'd get her hands into the dirt that day, fortune favored the prepared, so she had her favorite gardening gloves jammed in her back pocket. Most importantly, she had her notebook where she would begin to catalogue what was already in the garden and the plans that would elevate it all.

Alice felt a kinship with the sprawling estate's greenery that beckoned her forward. The garden before her was a patchwork of color and texture, with roses as its crown jewels. She meandered along the gravel paths, her hands brushing against the dewy softness of petals. An Omar Khayyam Rose caught her attention first, its deep pink blooms basking in the early light. Nearby, Ghislaine de Feligonde roses added a gentle contrast with their clustered blossoms that ranged from peach to pale yellow.

Alice paused beneath the trellis covered with Fantin de Latour roses, their ruffled blooms a soft pink, like the blush on her cheeks after an afternoon in the sun. They cascaded down in a fragrant waterfall, a living testament to the château's storied past. She admired them for a moment more, the artist in her reveling at the sight while the horticulturist considered the practicalities.

"Old friends," she whispered to the roses, her fingers tracing the gnarled wood of the supporting trellis. These varieties were venerable ones that had been around for decades, if not centuries. She took a moment to imagine the person who might have planted them here. Would they have imagined someone like Alice standing beneath them? Knowing their history and respecting what it meant? She hoped so. She often tried to imagine a person far in the future looking at her garden designs and understanding what she'd been trying to achieve. Even as she planned modern touches to invigorate the garden's design, she knew these heritage varieties would remain. They were a connection to the château's soul – a legacy that transcended time.

But challenges lay ahead. Alice found the hydrangeas, their scant blooms nodding gently in the morning breeze. Alice frowned slightly, pondering the soil's acidity levels. Roses thrived in it, yet René Dupont's desire for hydrangeas could be at odds with this preference. Hydrangeas were sensitive; their blooms could shift in hue if the pH balance wasn't just right. It was a delicate dance of chemistry and care, one that Alice knew all too well. She made a mental note to test the soil, considering how to accommodate both plants without compromising their beauty. Maybe that was what had made these particular hydrangeas suffer.

"Balance," she mused aloud, the word hanging in the air like a promise. Alice had built her reputation on achieving harmony in her designs. Harmony in color and placement and between the natural world and the busy world of modern life, between ornament and utility.. This garden would be no different. With tender care and meticulous planning, she would weave together the old and the new, creating a tapestry of flora that honored the château's history and welcomed its future.

Her fingers delved into the soil, feeling its warmth and texture, but as she surveyed the ornamental spread before her, she could see where changes could be made. Where were the rows of crisp lettuce, the trellises heavy with beans? The gardens boasted beauty but lacked the sustenance of a true cottage garden. She envisioned her hands stained with berry juice, not just dirt, and her the joy of eating a salad harvested from the grounds.

Water use was another factor. Provence had near drought conditions during most summers. She wanted to be sure she balanced the plants' needs with the environment's. The roses tended to need a good deal of water. Since she knew she wanted to keep them, some of the other more water-intensive plants would have to go.

"Time for a change," she declared to no one in particular, picturing neat rows of vegetables woven between the flower beds. She imagined the robust scent of herbs mingling with the delicate perfume of roses. In her mind's eye, persimmon trees offered dappled shade to underplantings of strawberries and mint. It was a vision of both bounty and beauty, rooted in practicality.

But then came the thought of honeybees. The hum of their industrious wings seemed to buzz at the edges of her imagination. Beehives would ensure pollination and yield sweet harvests, yet Alice couldn't help but hesitate. Would René have welcomed such companions in his vineyard domain? Maybe not. Some people were allergic. With a sigh, she tucked the idea away; perhaps it was a step too far, at least for now.

Pulling her straw hat down against the sun's warming rays, Alice settled onto a weathered bench, its wooden slats warmed from the day's early light. From her canvas bag, she drew out graph paper, a ruler, and colored pencils. The blank page beckoned, ready to start the transformation of the garden..

First, she sketched the main patio, envisioning it as the heart of future gatherings: guests laughing with glasses of René's finest in hand, the clink of bottles a melody against the chatter. Here, life would swirl around wine tastings and celebrations, a communal space that opened up from the château's welcoming arms.

From there, her pencil danced to the corners of the page, recording both what was already there and notations for creating alcoves of intimacy. A stone bench nestled under a weeping willow, a set of Adirondack chairs circled around a fire pit, a wrought-iron table set for two beside a bubbling fountain—each a private vignette for people to enjoy good company and good wine or a place for quiet reflection as they sipped. She could use some of the hedges as ways to create intimate areas. Some of it would have to go. She wasn't a big fan of yew. It was too stodgy for her, and the fact that it was toxic didn't endear it to her further. She wanted this garden to create sustenance for people, not poison them.

With each stroke, Alice infused the garden with potential, her design marrying the utility of edible plants with the existing splendor of the château's legacy. It was a plan that promised abundance and grace, where every leaf and petal played its part in a greater symphony of pastoral elegance.

"Voilà," she whispered, her eyes tracing over the colorful sketch. It was only a rough idea, but here was the beginning of transformation, a testament to the land's richness, the spirit of Provence and the enduring essence of growth.

She should consult with the winery's cook before finalizing the herbs, vegetables, and fruits she was planning. She hadn't met whoever that was yet. She should probably ask Lilou for information or perhaps René over dinner. She'd been too tired the night before to do much besides nod and listen.

Alice's pencil sketched more touches to her garden blueprints, a symphony of lines and shades that promised a future lush with greenery and life. The morning sun cast a warm glow over the parchment, illuminating her vision for a reinvented Eden at the château. Her focus was absolute, the world reduced to the paper before her and the plants that would soon rise from her meticulous planning.

"Planning a new paradise?" The voice, playful and rich, cut through Alice's concentration like a gentle breeze. She looked up, shading her eyes against the sunlight to see Marco Bellamy leaning against the gate, his dark hair tousled and a teasing smile playing on his lips. He wore jeans and an untucked button-down shirt rather than the chef's whites she was used to seeing him in. He looked relaxed and happy, and her heart leapt. For a second, she thought maybe she was imagining him.

"Marco!" Alice exclaimed, letting her papers and pencils fall to the ground as she rushed toward him. "What are you doing here in France?"

"Couldn't stay away from your charm," he joked, stepping closer and enveloping her in a hug.

Alice inhaled deeply, savoring that special herby smell that was quintessentially Marco and enjoying the feel of his strong arms around her.

Marco broke the hug and held her at arm's length, his brown eyes scanning her from head to foot. "You look beautiful as always, little blossom."

Alice felt a blush creep across her cheeks, an involuntary smile tugging at her lips. "Marco, I'm wearing overalls and clogs." And almost no makeup. She knew she should have taken a second to at least put on mascara that morning.

"With the way you make them look, you might set a new trend. Gardening chic."

They both laughed, but as the laughter died away, the air filled with hesitancy, both of them unsure how to bridge the gap formed by time apart despite the tether of messages and calls that had kept their connection alive. It was different to be together in the flesh.

"Did you get my text about the wild thyme I found in Crete?" Marco finally said, bridging the distance with a topic close to both their hearts.

"Yes, I did," Alice responded, warmth seeping into her tone as shared passions reignited the spark between them. "I can't wait to hear more about it."

A few more exchanges, each word delicately plucking at the strings of familiarity, brought them closer until they stood mere inches apart. Marco pulled her to him again, and this time, he kissed her. Their lips met, tentative at first, but growing bolder with each heartbeat. A current ran through them, igniting a memory of kisses past, a confluence of longing and affection. In that kiss, all the emails and texts paled in comparison to the undeniable truth of their chemistry. Alice lost herself in the warmth and taste of his kiss.

"God, I've missed this," Marco whispered, his voice barely louder than the rustling leaves around them.

"Me too," Alice admitted, her breath catching as Marco cupped her chin, his hand both strong and tender. "Now tell me, what are you really doing here?"

CHAPTER THREE

Marco stepped back just enough so Alice didn't have to crane her neck to look up at him. "DuPont contacted me. He wants to pair each wine in the rosé competition with a complementary dish inspired by the Provencal region and containing at least some locally grown ingredients. The concept is to enhance both the flavors of the wine and the food. He knew we were acquainted and asked what I thought about working with you."

"And?" Alice prompted.

"I said I would rather work with you than anyone else on earth." He smiled down at her. "I also asked him to keep it a secret so I could surprise you."

"Well, you definitely accomplished that!" Alice leaned her forehead against his broad chest. She loved the idea of combining the sensory experiences of taste and scent, blending the craft of vintner and chef and botanist into a harmonious symphony for the palate. The garden around them, with its lush vines and blooming flowers, seemed the perfect setting for such a collaboration.

"Sounds like a fun undertaking," she said, imagining the endless possibilities that could stem from such an endeavor.

"Yes," he replied, "and I thought it would be the perfect opportunity to work alongside you again." His brown eyes met hers, warm and inviting.

Marco's unexpected arrival was like a ray of sunlight piercing through the clouds of isolation that sometimes shrouded her during these projects. Despite her love for her work, the distance from home and family often left her with a pang of loneliness, especially during the quiet evenings after the day's bustle had died down. "I'm glad you're here."

His smile widened, and Alice couldn't help but notice how the garden seemed to come even more alive with him in it. His love for the earth's bounty matched her own; it was one of the many threads that drew her to him.

"René knew exactly how to lure me here," Marco said. "Springtime in Provence with a beautiful, intelligent woman at my side? I couldn't imagine saying no."

Alice nodded, as the sun warmed her face and the promise of new creations lay before them. "Then let's make sure we honor his vision," she said, meeting Marco's gaze. "Together."

"Exactly what I was hoping you'd say," Marco replied.

"Marco," she began, her voice steady but soft, "I can't tell you how much it means to have you here." She looked up at him, the corners of her mouth lifting into a smile. "This place, it's beautiful, but any place can feel lonely sometimes."

He pulled her closer. "I know what you mean," he said, his voice warm and comforting. "But I'm here now, and we're going to make this project something special. This time without any mysteries to distract us."

Alice's smile grew. The thought of having someone who shared her passions and understood the nuances of her work made the vast winery garden feel more intimate, as if they were in their own secluded world. It was exactly the kind of experience she wanted to create for other people. With Marco there, the long days wouldn't just be fulfilling; they'd be filled with laughter and companionship. Her solo ventures now felt like a prelude to this unexpected duet.

Turning her attention back to the garden, Alice let out a contented sigh. "Remember when we planned that kitchen garden back in Italy?" She caught Marco's eye, nostalgia tinting her voice. "We had such grand ideas for it."

"Ah, yes," Marco replied with a chuckle. "The herbs, the tomatoes... It was going to be magnificent." He brushed a stray leaf from one of the vines, his movements gentle and precise.

"Such a shame we never saw it come to life." Alice frowned slightly, her gaze drifting over the lush greenery around them.

"Maybe we didn't then," Marco said, the excitement clear in his tone. "But here we are, with another chance. This time, we'll see it through." His eyes gleamed with the promise of creation, igniting a spark within Alice.

She nodded, her heart buoyed by the prospect. The memory of their Italian dream, once dormant, now sprouted anew, the seeds of possibility taking root in the fertile ground of the winery's garden. With Marco by her side, the past disappointment transformed into fresh opportunity. They would nurture this new project together, and perhaps, in doing so, also cultivate the burgeoning connection between them.

Alice's mind teemed with ideas as she surveyed the patch of earth that would soon become their joint creation. "What do you think we should start with?" she asked Marco, eager to hear his culinary plans.

"Of course, I've been thinking about it," he laughed, the sound blending harmoniously with the soft rustle of the leaves around them. He leaned closer, his brown eyes alight with enthusiasm. "I want to try a deconstructed salad niçoise. Imagine fresh haricots vests, perfectly ripe cherry tomatoes, and some tiny, flavorful olives from the locals groves."

Alice's remembered the caprese skewers he had crafted back in Italy—bite-sized bursts of freshness that had danced on her tongue. "Those caprese skewers were divine," she mused aloud. "But there was something, a hidden note beneath the basil and balsamic..." She paused, considering, her eyes opening wide. "Was it thyme?"

"Spot on," Marco said, nodding approvingly. "You always had an impeccable palate."

Her cheeks flushed with a hint of pride. To have her taste recognized by someone as versed in flavors as Marco was a validation of her sensory talents. "Thyme has such a lovely, subtle earthiness. It'll be perfect for our garden here. Do you want to try the Greek variety you found?"

"Absolutely," Marco agreed. " I was also thinking about grilled vegetables with a pistou. It's a traditional Provencal dish that would pair wonderfully with René's wines."

"Grilled vegetables sound amazing," Alice replied, already envisioning the vibrant colors and smoky aromas that would fill the air. "And you're right, basil is essential. It's the soul of the pistou." She bent down, gently touching the soil, feeling its cool promise against her skin. "We'll need plenty of it. Sweet Genovese, or perhaps a hint of Purple Ruffles for contrast?"

"Both," Marco said with a decisive nod. "You bring the beauty to these projects, Alice. The way you combine aesthetics with practicality—it's art."

She looked up, meeting his gaze, and felt a warmth spread through her. Their collaboration was more than just plants and flavors; it was a mingling of passion and expertise, a shared love for the natural world that went beyond the mere cultivation of gardens or the crafting of dishes. Here in this winery's embrace, they were creating something tangible and alive—a testament to sustainable growth and the harmony of companionship.

It was so different than the connection she'd had with Scott all those years before. Marco looked at plants the same way she did. They weren't a means to a payout. They were their own end, full of beauty and flavor.

Alice leaned in closer to a cluster of lavender, her fingertips brushing against the delicate flowers as she inhaled their scent. "We'll need something to complement the herbs," she said, straightening up and turning toward Marco. "What about edible flowers? Which of your favorites we should include?"

Marco's eyes sparkled with enthusiasm. "Ah, violets would be wonderful. Their subtle sweetness could work marvels in a salad. And let's not forget squash. I can harvest some of the blossoms. Stuffed with ricotta and herbs, they're divine. Then later we'll have the vegetables themselves. They're fantastic on a grill."

"Perfect choices," Alice agreed, jotting down notes in her leather-bound journal.

"Plus," Marco continued, gesturing around the garden, "there's an abundance of roses here. We can infuse their petals into desserts or freeze them into ice cubes. Every variety offers a different flavor profile." He plucked a pale pink petal and held it out to her.

Alice took the petal, rolling it between her fingers before pressing it to her lips, tasting the subtle hint of sweetness. "I've always loved the idea of roses in cooking," she admitted. The notion reminded her of old-fashioned gardens and handwritten recipe books, of simpler times and pure flavors. Marco had a way of bringing those timeless elements into his dishes, making each bite both a memory and a discovery.

"Imagine a rose petal jam," he mused, "served with fresh scones or as a glaze for duck. The possibilities are endless."

"Stop! You're going to make me drool!" Alice laughed.

As they moved through the garden, discussing the potential uses for each plant, Alice felt a familiar flutter in her chest. She watched Marco, his hands animatedly sketching invisible dishes in the air as he spoke. His passion for his craft was one of the many things that drew her to him. It mirrored her own love for plants and design, creating a tapestry of mutual understanding and respect.

"Working on this garden with you..." she began, pausing to choose her words. "It feels like we're weaving together more than just plants and flavors. It's like we're blending our visions into something that's uniquely ours."

"Exactly," Marco replied, his dark eyes meeting hers with an intensity that made her heart skip. "Creating with you is like discovering a new language, one where every seed and spice tells a part of our story."

The late morning sun bathed them in golden light, lending the moment a glow that seemed to come from within as much as from without. Alice remembered the ease with which they'd planned the kitchen garden in Italy and how the project had been a harmonious mixture of their talents. Now, standing with him among the vines and scents of the winery's garden, she realized that the seeds of that unfinished Italian dream were ready to bloom anew in this fertile ground.

"Marco," she said softly, the word itself feeling like a promise, "I think we're going to create something really special here."

He reached out, his hand gently touching hers. "With you, Alice, I have no doubt that we will."

CHAPTER FOUR

Any more discussion of gardens and partnerships was halted by Lilou coming out to tell them that lunch was ready.

Alice and Marco followed her into the kitchen where they washed their hands and then into the dining room of the château, her senses instantly awakened by the warm and rustic scents of rosemary and thyme. The long wooden table was set with an elegance that spoke of tradition without pretense. Sunlight danced through the windows, casting a natural spotlight on the centerpiece—a crystal decanter filled with a blush-colored wine.

"Marco!" René welcomed him with open arms and a kiss on each cheek. "I didn't know you had arrived!"

"Only a few minutes ago." Marco gestured to Alice. "Mademoiselle Bloom and I got engrossed in discussing the garden and how it might work for me and for you. We forgot about everything else."

"Excellent," René said. "Exactly what I hoped would happen. I knew your philosophies would work well together. Have you met my assistant Sophie?"

Sophie once again looked impossibly elegant for someone wearing work clothes. She extended a hand and Marco shook it. "Enchanté," he said.

"Likewise," Sophie said with a smile. "I'm looking forward to seeing what you will cook up. René has been excited about your arrival."

"Yes, yes." René waved her words away as if he was embarrassed. "Please, everyone, sit."

Alice sat on René's left and Marco on his right with Sophie on the other side of Marco. Jean-Baptiste sat next to Alice and Lilou took a spot at the foot of the table. "The table looks beautiful," Alice said.

Lilou acknowledged the compliment with a smile and returned to the kitchen.

"Voilà," René announced with pride, picking up the decanter and pouring the rosé into their glasses. "This vintage is in honor of my mother, a woman as delicate yet spirited as this wine."

"Cheers to her," Marco raised his glass. "And to mothers

everywhere."

They toasted, and the wine tasted like summer gardens and whispered secrets between lovers, cool and refreshing with an ever so slight lingering sweetness. Alice was entranced with it, taking small sips and holding them in her mouth to try to capture all the different notes she was tasting. As the lunch unfolded with plates of ratatouille and tender coq au vin, conversation turned seamlessly from the flavors on their tongues to the garden outside.

"René, Marco and I were talking about integrating some edible flowers among the plants—perhaps nasturtiums or violets," Alice suggested, her mind painting the garden's palette.

"Interesting," Rene mused, swirling his glass contemplatively. "And Marco, your expertise would complement this idea beautifully."

"Absolutely," Marco chimed in, leaning forward with enthusiasm. "I can envision dishes infused with these same botanicals, echoing the landscape on the plate."

"Harmony in the glass and on the plate," Alice smiled, pleased at the collaboration taking shape before them. They spent the remainder of their meal weaving ideas together until it felt like the garden itself had joined them at the table, lush and vibrant in its future potential.

The clink of cutlery and the final sips of rosé marked the end of the leisurely lunch. Sophie excused herself to oversee something in the wine cellars. "I need to be certain the rosé is both heat and cold stable. We'll be bottling soon and we'll need to correct any issues before then."

"Yes. Make sure the malic acid levels are at least 150," René said, nodding.

"You mean under 100, don't you?" Sophie asked, getting up from the table.

René frowned. "I don't think so." He waved her away. "We can discuss it later."

Lilou and Jean-Baptiste exchanged a look that Alice couldn't quite interpret.

"I'd love to see the cellars," Alice said.

"Certainly, I can arrange a tour," Sophie said, glancing over at René. "If it's okay with Monsieur DuPont."

"Mais oui," he said. "I should have arranged that already."

"I'd love to tag along if I could," Marco said.

"Absolutely. Right now I need to see to some tasks. How about tomorrow morning?" Sophie offered.

"Excellent," Alice said. "Thank you.

After Sophie left, Alice excused herself also, keen to capture the inspiration that the shared vision had ignited within her. She stepped out onto the terrace, notebook in hand, ready to transpose their ideas onto paper before she forgot them.

As she walked along the gravel path towards the beds of hydrangeas, Alice noted the sunlight dappling through the leaves, playing tricks with the colors. She stopped, crouching down to inspect the blooms more closely. The hydrangeas, once decidedly pink, were now exhibiting hints of periwinkle blue at their edges. The flowers themselves were small and sparse.

"Curious," Alice murmured to herself, feeling the first stirrings of concern. René's casual demeanor suggested he might not notice such subtleties, but to Alice, this was a sign—a whisper of change that could not be overlooked. She reached out, her fingers brushing against the soft petals as if they held answers to the quiet question stirring in her heart.

"Could the soil be changing?" she pondered aloud, though only the flowers kept her company. A change in pH was the likely culprit for the color change, but what could cause such a shift?

Alice knelt beside the hydrangeas and parted the foliage to get a closer look at the soil. She furrowed her brow, thoughts ticking like clockwork beneath her sunhat. The change in color from pink to blue was not a trivial matter for a plant enthusiast like herself—it was a clue, a riddle that beckoned to be solved.

First step would be to make sure she was right in her assumptions about the pH levels. She stood, tapping her index finger against her lower lip and thinking. She had yet to start gathering supplies, so she didn't have a pH testing kit. There were ways around that, though.

She went back to the kitchen where Marco and Lilou were discussing what groceries would be needed and a schedule for the kitchen.

"Marco, Lilou," she said, "do you have vinegar and baking soda?"

Lilou nodded. "Of course, Mademoiselle Alice. What kind of vinegar? White wine? Red wine? Balsamic?"

Alice laughed. "Nothing so fancy. Apple cider or plain white?"

"Give me a moment," Lilou said as she left the kitchen. "The white vinegar is kept with the cleaning supplies."

While Lilou went to get the vinegar, Alice rummaged through the cabinets to find two containers. Lilou returned with the jug of vinegar and pulled a container of baking soda from another cabinet. "If I may ask, what is it we're doing with these items?"

"I'll show you." Alice picked up the items and beckoned for them to follow her to the garden and led them to the hydrangeas.

Marco, with an ever-curious glint in his brown eyes, exchanged a glance with Lilou, and then looked back to Alice. "Are we having a science class in the garden?"

"Sort of," Alice replied with a half-smile, setting up her supplies. "I don't have my pH kit with me, so I'm going back to basics—high school chemistry."

She sprinkled a handful of soil into one of the containers and formed a small well in the center before adding a splash of vinegar. Nothing happened. She picked up the container and held it close to her ear. No reaction. Next, she mixed another sample with a bit of water and then added baking soda to it. The mixture fizzed and bubbled, confirming her suspicion.

"Acidic soil," she announced, looking up at their bemused faces. "That's what's turning the hydrangeas blue. It might explain why they look so bedraggled, too, although I'm not sure about that."

"Wow, I didn't realize you could test soil like that," Marco said, genuinely impressed.

"Neither did I," admitted Lilou, her eyes wide.

Alice felt a flutter of pride at their admiration but pushed it aside. There were larger concerns at hand. What could be causing such a drastic shift in the soil's acidity? Was it only here by the hydrangeas?

"Let's check out a few other places in the garden." She took her supplies and went over to where lavender plants marched along a straight walkway. The soil there wasn't acidic.

She moved next to one of the yew hedges. Again, the soil didn't test as acidic.

"It's like watching a detective at work." Lilou said.

"A thorough and very intelligent detective," Marco added.

"Thank you both," she said, dusting off her hands. "But I need to make a call. It's time to consult an expert on this matter."

Leaving the hydrangeas behind, Alice found a quiet spot under an old apple tree whose branches bore the first blush of spring. She dialed the number for Dr. Lily Greenway, her mentor, who picked up after the third ring.

"Dr. Greenway, it's Alice Bloom. I hope I'm not interrupting."

"Never, dear," came the warm, crackling voice. "I always have time for you. What's on your mind?"

Alice explained the situation. "The hydrangeas in René's garden— they're changing color. I suspect the soil is becoming too acidic."

"Ah, hydrangeas, those delicate litmus papers of the garden." Dr. Greenway chuckled. "Let's go through the possibilities, shall we? Talk me through your observations, Alice. We'll get to the root of this together."

As Alice recounted her findings, she could almost picture Dr. Greenway nodding along, the retired professor's brain whirring into action despite the miles between them.

"Hydrangeas are quite sensitive to pH changes. An increase in acidity shifts their flowers from pink to blue. Now, as for why your soil's pH has spiked—natural causes are possible but rare. Could be excessive rainfall, decomposing organic matter, or even the parent material," Dr. Greenway said.

There'd been an average amount of rainfall for the past year and most of the soil in Provence was limestone and clay, which were generally less acidic than say granite.

Alice nodded to herself, tracing her finger over the knotted patterns of the tree bark beside her. "Even so, those wouldn't increase acidity overnight, would they? It seems too sudden, and it doesn't really explain why they seem less robust than the rest of the plants in the garden."

"Quite right, my dear. Spontaneous changes in soil chemistry are seldom that rapid without intervention. Nor are they usually so localized. My guess is this was done by someone adding too much of an ammonium nitrate fertilizer."

"That sounds deliberate," Alice said, not being able to imagine accidentally putting too much fertilizer onto the hydrangeas.

"Is there any reason someone would single out the hydrangeas?" Dr. Greenway asked.

"I'm not sure. I'm the only one who seemed to noticed the color change. René did mention they were his mother's favorites." She looked up into the branches of the tree overhead. Could someone have a grudge against René's mother? If so, why wait ten years to sabotage her favorite flowers? She shook her head. Maybe the why didn't matter. Maybe the only thing to worry about was how to fix it. "What should I do?"

"To neutralize the soil, you'll need to add lime. But the real question is not just how, but who and why someone would alter the soil intentionally."

"Exactly." The words felt heavy as they left Alice's lips. The thought of someone meddling with René's garden was more than an academic curiosity; it was personal.

"Keep me posted, Alice. And remember, a good detective looks beyond the obvious.

"Will do, Dr. Greenway. Thank you." She ended the call and remained seated under the apple tree, the later afternoon sun casting long shadows across the lawn.

***

Later, after the sky turned a deep shade of twilight, Alice lay in bed, staring at the ceiling. She had barely made it through dinner before her head began to nod. The candles on the table had sent a warm glow around them. Marco and Lilou had worked together on the meal and it was a lovely amalgamation of authentic Provencal cuisine with Marco's elevating touches and, of course, wine. It had been fascinating to sit next to Sophie and hear more of what she did as the assistant vintner and what went into making the rosé that had created even more of that golden glow. Her passion for winemaking came through in every word she said.

Now that Alice was tucked into bed, the quiet hum of the French countryside should have been a lullaby, but her mind buzzed with unanswered questions. Someone was intentionally tampering with the soil. Who would care enough about the color of hydrangeas to meddle with them? René said the hydrangeas were his mother's favorite, and he particularly wanted them to be part of the presentation of her rosé at the competition. Could that somehow be part of what was happening?

She rolled onto her side, the image of the garden etched behind her eyelids. René's mother had loved those hydrangeas. The change in hue felt like a violation of that memory, a slight against the legacy left behind. But why?

The wine, the food, the land—it all tied together. René's rosé, named after his mother, was a testament to tradition. Was someone trying to sabotage that? Or was the motive less sinister, something more prosaic hidden beneath layers of dirt and deceit?

As Alice finally drifted into a restless sleep, one thought lingered: changing the color of hydrangeas required knowledge and intent. This was no accident. It was a message, and she was determined to uncover its meaning.

CHAPTER FIVE

Alice stretched her arms towards the ceiling, letting out a soft yawn as the golden rays of dawn filtered through the curtains, painting the room in warm hues. She showered and put on a clean pair of overalls, then padded down the stairs, drawn by the rich aroma of freshly ground coffee that permeated the air. In the kitchen, Marco was a study of relaxed concentration, his broad shoulders bending as he pressed down the plunger of the French press.

Alice paused for a moment in the doorway to watch him. She was glad he was here for so many reasons. The way his muscles rippled under his shirt was just one of them. "Good morning," Alice said.

"Morning, Alice," Marco replied without turning, a smile in his voice. "I hope you like your coffee strong and your mornings sweet."

"Perfect combination," she said, taking a seat at the wide oak table where Marco served her a steaming cup and a flaky *pain au chocolat*. Such a French breakfast. Of course, Marco would know that and honor it.

"So, what's on your agenda today?" Marco asked, leaning against the counter with his own cup cradled between his hands.

"Actually, I wanted to look more into the soil composition around the gardens. I'm wondering if it's just the soil around the hydrangeas or if other areas of the grounds are affected, too." Alice took a sip, savoring the dark, rich blend before continuing. "But honestly, I'm open to anything that involves getting dirt under my fingernails."

"Always anxious to get to work." Marco chuckled, brushing a lock of dark hair from his eyes. "How about we take a walk through the vineyards later? Sophie mentioned there are some rare grape varieties I've been eager to see."

"Sounds wonderful." She didn't hate the idea of exploring the lush vines with Marco.

The kitchen door swung open, and Sophie stepped inside. "Bon matin!" she said, her eyes bright with enthusiasm. "Are you both free this morning? Would you like a tour of where the real magic happens at Château Dupont?"

"That would be delightful." Alice finished her coffee and wiped her mouth. The pain au chocolat had long since disappeared.

"Absolutely," Marco said, setting his now empty coffee cup down, too.

"Great! Follow me," Sophie said, leading them out of the kitchen and into the winery itself.

They walked past the stainless steel vats of the fermentation area, where Sophie explained the precise temperatures needed for each varietal. The laboratory was next, its gleaming surfaces and state-of-the-art equipment quite unexpected amidst the rustic charm of the château. Alice watched as Sophie handled the instruments with familiarity, demonstrating the tests that ensured the quality of each batch.

"Science meets tradition here," Sophie said with a hint of pride.

"And it results in exceptional wine," Marco added, admiring a device used for measuring sugar levels.

Their path continued into the barrel room, a cathedral-like space lined with rows of oak barrels. The scent of wood and aging wine hung heavy in the cool air, mingling with the musty undernotes of the château's ancient stones.

"Each barrel is a promise. Or maybe a dream of what's possible," Sophie remarked, her gaze sweeping over her charges.

Alice couldn't help but feel a tingle of reverence for the craft as she trailed her fingers over the smooth staves, wondering about the countless stories encapsulated within.

The final stop was the most breathtaking. They descended stone steps worn smooth by centuries of treading feet, arriving in the aging cellar. It was a cavernous room dug directly into the bedrock, a natural fortress for the bottles that slumbered in their racks.

"12th century," Sophie whispered, as if speaking too loudly might disturb the resting vintages. "It's not just a cellar; it's a time capsule."

"Amazing," Alice murmured, her voice echoing off the walls. The coolness of the rock seeped through her clothes, sending a shiver up her spine, but it wasn't unwelcoming. It was as though the earth itself embraced the essence of the winemaking process, protecting the legacy of the château.

"Shall we head back up?" Marco suggested after a moment of reverent silence, .

"Of course," Sophie agreed, leading the way back to the warmth of the sunlit world above.

The ascent from the hallowed subterranean wine sanctuary was like returning from another time. Alice's thoughts, however, couldn't stay rooted in the historical marvels Sophie had shown them for long.

"I wish I'd known about your lab yesterday," Alice said, as they emerged into Provence's dappled sunlight. "I spent yesterday afternoon testing soil acidity with vinegar and baking soda."

Sophie cocked her head to the side, curiosity lighting up her features. "Why were you doing that?"

"Ah, it's the hydrangeas," Alice replied, her voice carrying her concern. "They're shifting from pink to a blue—a clear sign of increased acidity in the soil."

A flicker of alarm passed over Sophie's face. "Acidic soil would be problematic for the grapevines, too," Sophie noted, her brow furrowing.

"Exactly," Alice agreed. "I'm worried about what could cause such a drastic change. It's not common for soil pH to shift so quickly without some sort of catalyst."

"Perhaps we should collect some samples together?" Sophie suggested. "We can use the lab equipment to get more precise readings."

"Thank you, that would be fantastic," Alice said. It would be great to have access to the lab and someone who was at least as well versed in soil composition as she was herself to work with. "I think something else might be happening there, too. I'm not sure what, though. A closer, more comprehensive look would help."

Their conversation was cut short by the sound of a vehicle pulling up to the château. Alice turned to see an SUV rolling to a stop near the front entrance. A Land Rover. Her heart skipped as she thought about the person she knew who always drove one of those no matter where he went. Surely it couldn't be him.

But it was.

Scott Thorne unfolded himself from the driver's seat, his tall and lanky frame straightening to its full height. His blond hair gleamed in the morning sun. He jammed a straw cowboy hat on his head as he looked around.

"Thorne," Marco said, his distaste evident in his voice.

"Who?" Sophie asked, looking from Marco to Alice.

"An... old acquaintance," Alice managed to say just as Scott's blue-eyed gaze landed on her.

"Ma fleur! I'd heard you were here!" he called out in that thick Louisiana drawl of his and started striding toward her.

Alice put her hands on her hips. "From who?" If she found who was feeding Scott Thorne information about her whereabouts, she'd . . . Well, she'd do something. She wasn't sure what yet, but something.

"And I'm not your flower."

He shook his head and chuckled as if she'd said something funny. "You will always be my flower, and you know how the plant world is. Talk talk talk." He held up his hand and made the blah blah gesture with it. He turned to Marco. "Chef Bellamy, nice to see you again."

Marco nodded, but didn't say anything. Alice doubted either of them were happy to see each other. They'd reached a sort of detente in Italy, but they were far from friends. "What are you doing here?" The difference she felt when she saw Marco unexpectedly to how she felt about unexpectedly seeing Scott hit her. There was a time when she didn't think she'd ever get over Scott. Everything had reminded her of him. Maybe she was finally past the heartache.

"Tracking down a rare orchid. Something pretty special. A hybrid of sorts. Should be worth quite the pretty penny," Scott said. "Heard rumors it might be around here. Also heard a rumor about a certain talented landscape designer staying at this château."

"Coincidences abound," Marco said dryly, stepping a little closer to Alice. His protective stance wasn't lost on her, and she felt a warmth that had nothing to do with the sun overhead.

"Is that so?" Alice responded, striving to keep her tone neutral. "Well, I hope your search is successful."

"Me too," Scott said, glancing around the estate with an appraiser's eye. "It's quite the place you've found yourself in."

"It is," Alice replied in a tone she hoped would put an end to conversation. "Scott, this is Sophie Moreau."

Scott removed his straw cowboy hat with his left hand and stuck out his right. "Very pleased to meet you, miss."

Alice wasn't sure she believed Scott's excuse. His arrival was as unexpected as a frost in May and equally unwelcome as far as she was concerned. She couldn't quite shake the feeling that his professed quest for a rare orchid was little more than a cover story, but for what? She thought she'd made her feelings — or lack thereof — very clear at the end of their adventures in Italy. Confrontation was the last thing she wanted, though.

"Enchanté," Sophie greeted him, her French accent making the world melodic.

"Ooh," Scott said, a slow smile spreading across his face. "I like the way you say that."

Sophie gave a slight bow of her head. "You say you're here seeking an orchid? For what reason?"

Scott braced one foot on a small boulder that marked the edge of the driveway. "It's my business. I'm an orchid hunter."

Sophie's eyes went wide. "An orchid hunter? That sounds quite adventurous."

"Part of the job's charm," Scott replied, his voice smooth as polished stone. He had yet to relinquish Sophie's hand.

"I'd love to hear more about it," Sophie said, seemingly happy to have her hand in Scott's.

"I'd be happy to tell you about it." He launched into an explanation of his work, discussing the delicate ecosystems that housed such treasures. Alice could see Sophie's polite interest, perhaps even genuine curiosity, flicker in her eyes like candlelight.

Seizing the moment, Alice excused herself with a murmured intention to revisit the hydrangeas. As she walked away from Scott's animated storytelling and Sophie's attentive listening, the knot in her stomach began to loosen. Maybe Scott would get the hint and leave. Or maybe he'd transfer some of his interest to Sophie and leave Alice alone. Either was fine with her.

The garden welcomed her with open arms, the sun had risen higher and the garden looked almost like a painting, with everything thrown into high contrast. It was here among these living things that Alice felt most at home, with the soil beneath her fingernails. Plants had been what had helped her get over her broken heart. They'd always been there for her and she did her best to be there for them.

She knelt by the hydrangeas, their petals a mosaic of blues and pinks, a visual representation of the soil's subtle shifts in pH levels. As she examined the plants, looking for any signs of distress, she froze. There, lying amongst the roots and fallen leaves, was René Dupont. His body was still, too still, and his eyes stared vacantly at the sky above. His skin looked blue.

She scrambled to her feet. "René!" Alice gasped, her voice strangled in her throat. Her scream followed, piercing the morning calm and sending birds scattering from the trees.

Footsteps thudded against the earth as Marco, Scott, Sophie, Jean-Baptiste, and Lilou converged on the scene. Marco reached Alice first, his broad shoulders blocking out the sight of René as he pulled her into an embrace and away from the grisly discovery.

"I will call for help," Lilou said, her voice shaking uncharacteristically, although Alice didn't think there was much help anyone could offer to René anymore.

"Mon Dieu," Sophie murmured under her breath, one hand covering her mouth in shock. She took two steps back.

"Is he...?" Scott began, but couldn't finish the question.

Alice clung to Marco, her head buried in his chest, as he whispered comforting nothings into her hair. She lifted her face to his, her eyes brimming with tears.

"Not again," she whispered back, the weight of déjà vu pressing down on her. Once more, death had found its way into her life, turning the beauty of nature into a backdrop for tragedy.

CHAPTER SIX

Alice shivered, although the château's kitchen was warm. Marco grabbed a throw and wrapped it around her shoulders before handing her a steaming cup of sweet milky tea. The warmth seeped through the fine china, comforting in its familiarity. She wrapped her fingers around the cup, grateful for something to hold onto.

She shut her eyes, trying to calm herself. *Make a list. It's springtime. Ephemeral plants. Daffodil. Jack-in-the Pulpit. Eastern Shooting Star. Trilliums. Hyacinth.* The names of the plants soothed her like putting on a familiar sweater.

"Better?" Marco asked.

She opened her eyes to find his eyes searching hers with genuine concern.

"Much better, thank you," she managed a small smile, feeling the heat begin to thaw her frozen insides and the shivers slow down.

He nodded. "The British aren't wrong about everything culinary. Sometimes a cup of hot tea is exactly what's required."

She huffed a small laugh and took another sip of the tea.

Sophie and Scott entered the kitchen, Sophie's face pale and drawn. Scott hovered close behind her, offering quiet words that seemed to go unheard. Sophie sat down at the table opposite Alice and put her face in her hands. "Mon Dieu. I can't believe this is happening."

"Where's Lilou?" Marco asked, preparing another cup of tea.

"She's insisting on staying with . . . the body until emergency services arrive," Sophie said looking up and then seeming almost to gag a little. "What do you think happened to him? Could it be a heart attack? He looked so wrong."

"Did he have heart problems?" Alice asked. He'd seemed so healthy and vital.

"Not that I know of." Sophie shook her head. "Why was he blue?"

Scott put his hand on Sophie's shoulder. "That's for the police to figure out."

Marco put another cup of sweet milky tea down in front of Sophie, then leaned back against the kitchen counter, arms crossed over his chest. He did not offer Scott a cup of tea, but if Scott noticed he didn't say anything.

The group fell silent. The silence between them all punctuated only by the distant ticking of the grandfather clock until a sharp rap at the door broke it. A man entered without waiting to be invited.

"Bonjour," he said, bowing his head slightly. "I am Inspector Pierre Fournier. I will need to speak with each of you separately," he announced in a tone that brokered no argument.

He was a tall man, taller even than Marco, who stood a little over six feet. Fournier had a strong jawline and sharp features. White with dark hair, he wore combed back from his forehead and gelled into place. He had on a dark suit, crisply pressed, and a neatly knotted tie. He looked like a bad guy in a film about the 1980s.

Fournier's gaze swept the room and landed on Alice. "Mademoiselle Bloom?" he asked.

Alice nodded.

"If you would join me first?" Alice set her tea down with a careful thunk against the wooden table and followed Fournier to the adjoining parlor. The scent of expensive cologne followed the Inspector, a subtle aroma of cedar and spices .

Once they were seated, he took out a pen and a notepad and asked, "Please, tell me what brings you to Château DuPont." His voice was smooth and measured, his words were punctuated by the faint clicking of his pen as he waited for Alice's answer.

"First, can you tell me what happened to Monsieur DuPont?" Alice asked. "Do you know?"

Fournier pressed his lips together as if to seal them and then said, "There will be an autopsy. That will tell us what happened."

Alice slumped back in the chair. "So no chance that he had a heart attack or something like that?"

Fournier clicked his pen a few times and then finally said, "It seems doubtful. Poison seems more likely."

"Poison?" Alice's hand went to her heart.

"Possibly." Fournier clicked his pen a few times. "Now, please tell me how you came to be at Château Fournier."

"Monsieur DuPont hired the landscaping firm I work for to redesign his garden." Alice looked down at a smear of dirt on her hands that she hadn't noticed. "I was here to consult with him, draw up plans, and begin the implementation of the design. René had a vision for the gardens here. He wanted something a little less formal, but still elegant. An elevated cottage garden really. He also wanted to honor his mother. He's presenting a rosé named after her in a competition and he wanted there to be special places in the garden honoring her as well."

"Such as?"

"Well, the hydrangeas, of course."

"Ah, yes, the hydrangeas. Where you found Monsieur DuPont. Interesting." Fournier nodded, jotting down notes. "And how did you plan to implement Monsieur Dupont's vision?"

"Through a careful selection of plant varieties, soil analysis, and a layout that would complement the estate's architecture and history." Alice's passion for her work bloomed in her chest, a welcome respite from the morning's dark events. "It's about creating a harmony between the cultivated and the wild, a place where both can prosper. We want to make the garden reflect the long history of Château DuPont, but also look to the future."

"Is that so?" Fournier murmured, his pen pausing for just a moment. "And this work, it was important to you?"

"Very much so," Alice said, holding Fournier's gaze. "Gardens are more than just aesthetics, they're a legacy. I wanted to honor René's wishes and make the château's grounds a testament to his vision and his mother's memory."

Fournier considered her words, the ghost of a smile touching the corner of his mouth before he returned to his methodical questioning. Alice sensed the shift back to the matter at hand, the brief interlude of talking about her craft dissolving into the stark reality of the investigation that lay before them.

"Mademoiselle Bloom," Fournier began, his voice steady, "were there any issues between you and Monsieur Dupont?"

Alice blinked a few times, surprised at the question. "No, Inspector. I only arrived a couple of days ago. We had barely even gotten started. There hadn't been time for any kind of issues to arise, and nothing I saw in my short time here made me think there would be."

Fournier's eyebrow arched ever so slightly, a silent question lingering in the skepticism of his gaze. He made a note in his little black book, the sound of pen scratching on paper filling the brief void.

"And when was the last time you saw Monsieur Dupont alive?" he asked, looking up again.

Alice released a slow breath, her mind casting back over the last day. She rocked a little in her seat as she thought. Had she seen him this morning? No. She was sure not. She'd come down to the kitchen and then Sophie had taken them on the tour of the winery. "It was at dinner last night." Her voice held steady, even as her heart twinged with the recollection of how golden and beautiful the evening had seemed to her and what a shadow this morning had cast over it

"Who else was present?"

"René, Sophie, Marco, Lilou, Jean-Baptiste, and myself," she recounted smoothly, each name evoking a face, a smile, an exchanged glance from the night that now seemed worlds away.

"Did anything unusual occur? An argument, perhaps?" Fournier's question was casual, but his eyes were sharp, missing nothing.

She shook her head. "Not at all. It was a lovely dinner. We celebrated the day's progress in the gardens, discussed the next steps in the rosé's evolution. It was very pleasant," she insisted, but a trace of uncertainty fluttered in her chest. Had there been a shadow in someone's eye she hadn't noticed? There'd been those little glances between Lilou and Jean-Baptiste. Did they mean something?

Fournier made a note. "Mademoiselle Bloom," he began, his voice as smooth, "you went directly to the hydrangeas where Monsieur DuPont was found this morning. Can you explain why?"

Alice nodded, clasping her hands to still their slight tremble. "Of course, Inspector. The hydrangeas—they've been changing color. It's not the seasonal shift one would expect. They're turning a deep shade of blue, indicative of acidic soil. They also don't seem to be growing as they should. I'm trying to figure out why."

"Go on," Fournier prompted, the click of his pen pausing.

"Hydrangeas change color based on the pH level of the soil," she explained, happy to talk about something definite, something she knew to be true. "I was concerned that something—or someone—may have altered the soil composition in that area deliberately."

"Deliberately?" Fournier echoed, his brow furrowing. "Why would someone do that?"

Alice shook her head. "I wish I knew. It's perplexing. Hydrangeas are resilient, but such a sudden shift... it could harm them, or be a sign of something more malicious at play. I only noticed it yesterday. That's why I wanted to check them this morning."

Fournier scribbled a note, then met her eyes again. "Thank you, Mademoiselle. That will be all for now. Please refrain from discussing this matter with the others until I've completed my interviews."

"Of course, Inspector," Alice replied, relief blooming within her chest. She rose from the chair, feeling the tension in her shoulders ease. As she moved towards the door, she thought, *At least he hasn't told me not to leave the country.*

"Ah, and one more thing," Fournier called out just as her hand touched the doorknob.

Alice turned, her heart skipping a beat.

"Please stay available and do not consider leaving France until this investigation is concluded," he stated, his tone carrying the weight of authority.

Her stomach dropped. So much for small favors, recalling the stern warnings of Italian authorities from her past misadventure.

"Inspector Fournier, am I a suspect?" She might as well know the truth.

He shrugged. "You are new. You arrived, and someone died soon after. You found the body. And I understand this isn't the first time one of your clients has died in a less than natural way."

With a nod of understanding to Fournier, Alice stepped out of the kitchen, the specter of suspicion trailing close behind.

CHAPTER SEVEN

Alice trudged up the narrow staircase, the worn treads creaking beneath her feet. Her mind churned like the soil she so often worked, thoughts of René DuPont's untimely demise mingling with unexpected encounters. The quaint charm of her room offered little solace as she shut the door behind her. She reached for her phone, its sleek surface cool and unyielding in her palm.

"Jazz, it's Alice," she said when the call connected, her voice a blend of sadness and urgency. She didn't waste any time getting the words out. "DuPont's dead."

"Wait! What?" Jazz's tone was laden with shock, the background hum of her tea shop receding as if pushed away by the gravity of the news. "Dead? But how?

"I don't know yet. The police won't say, but they're definitely treating it like it's not a natural death. The Inspector mentioned that they suspected poison." Alice perched on the edge of the bed, the antique quilt offering no comfort. "I found him in the hydrangeas." She couldn't stop the little sob from escaping at the thought of how he'd looked, so cold and alone.

"Murder?" Jazz echoed, her voice a cocktail of concern and disbelief. "I thought your days of stumbling upon bodies were behind you."

"Me too," Alice murmured. The memory of Italy's sun-drenched coast flashed across her mind, but she pushed it aside. "There's more. Marco arrived yesterday."

"Marco is there?" Jazz sounded surprised, but also a bit excited. "That's a twist. What's he doing there?"

"DuPont hired him to create a menu for an upcoming rosé competition based on what grows here. Kind of a local-vore thing." She paused, not sure what was going to happen to the project. "We were going to work together so what I planted and what he created for the menu would go hand-in-hand." And maybe, just maybe, she and Marco could go hand in hand as well?

"Of all the gardens in all the towns in all the world." Jazz in a terrible Humphrey Bogart imitation. "Seriously, though. How was that?"

"Not bad. A little awkward at first, but then it felt like we were picking back up right where we left off." Alice's hand went to her mouth to touch the place he'd kissed her. "Until this morning when Scott showed up."

"Scott? Again? What is he even doing there?" Jazz's bewilderment mirrored Alice's own.

"Orchid hunting, or so he says." Alice ran a hand through her hair. "I can't deal with him right now, not with all this. I hope having the police question him about a murder will be enough to scare him off."

"Come home, Alice," Jazz urged, her voice urgent. "You don't need to be caught up in another mess. Last time, you almost died."

"Home sounds good," Alice admitted, gazing out the window at the expansive gardens, now tainted with the shadow of death. She was well aware of the close call she'd had in Italy. "But I can't, not yet."

"Don't tell me." Jazz sighed. "You've been told not to leave the country."

"Got it in one." Alice sat down and fell back onto the bed, staring up at the ceiling as if there might be answers there. "Apparently, finding DuPont makes me part of this mess and Inspector Fournier brought up Italy."

"Seriously? You were cleared in that case. It was all over the papers," Jazz protested, her tone sharpening like the shears Alice used to prune her beloved roses.

"I know, and you know, but I'm not convinced Fournier sees it that way." She sat back up, pulling her legs up to sit tailor-style. "Jazz, do you think there's any chance DuPont's death is linked to the hydrangea color change?"

"The what now?" Jazz asked.

Alice filled her in on the acidic soil around the hydrangeas and her concern that there was more going awry there that she hadn't quite figured out yet.

"Me? I'm all about herbs and teas, remember?" Jazz chuckled lightly on the other end. "You're the plant guru. What's your take?"

"Hydrangeas shift hues based on soil pH," Alice mused aloud, the detective in her surfacing. "But it would be extraordinary if someone manipulated them on purpose... and for what? And what about that would lead to someone poisoning René? Unless..."

"Unless DuPont stumbled onto something he wasn't supposed to?" Jazz offered.

"Exactly," Alice replied, feeling the familiar thrill of piecing together a botanical puzzle. "It's just speculation right now, but I can't ignore the timing."

"Be careful, Alice," Jazz warned, her voice taking on a serious note. "Remember, you're not there to play detective."

"Understood." Alice sighed, the weight of concern from her friend making her promise herself an extra measure of caution. "I'll talk to you soon, Jazz."

"Stay safe, okay? And keep me posted." Jazz's concern was palpable even from across the globe.

"Will do," Alice promised before ending the call. She sat for a moment longer, the silence of the room pressing against her. She had one more call to make. She took a deep breath and blew it out, then hit the button to call her boss. Owen answered on the second ring, his voice carrying the usual blend of gruff concern. "Bloom, how's Provence?"

"Beautiful, but there's a problem." Her finger traced the pattern on the bedspread.

"What kind of problem?"

"René DuPont is dead. I found him in the hydrangeas this morning and the police are treating it as a suspicious death." She said the words quickly as if she could somehow sneak them by Owen.

There was a pause and then a very gusty sigh. "Not again, Bloom. Not again."

She almost laughed. "That was my reaction exactly, Owen."

"Any idea of what will happen to the project?"

That was Owen all over, always focused on the business. "None. I'll let you know as soon as I know anything."

"See that you do," Owen grumbled, though Alice could hear his concern grow. "Stay out of harm's way, Alice. Please."

"Will do," she assured him before ending the call.

Alice's stomach growled. She looked at her watch. Breakfast had been hours ago. She'd been too upset to think about being hungry before. She was calmer now after talking to Jazz and Owen. Surely no one would mind if she crept down to the kitchen to get a little snack? She left her room and made her way back down the narrow stairs. As she descended, the murmur of voices grew louder, until she could discern words, then heated exchanges.

"Marco, I need answers!" Inspector Fournier's voice was stern and unyielding. "And I need them now!"

"Inspector, I've told you everything I know," Marco replied, his warm tone strained with frustration.

Alice paused mid-step, her heart skipping a beat at the sound of Marco's voice. She leaned against the cool wood of the banister, the grain pressing into her palm. She knew she shouldn't eavesdrop, but she couldn't help herself. The urge to know, to understand, to protect Marco, perhaps, rooted her to the spot. She held her breath, listening.

Alice inched closer to the top of the landing, her fingers tightening around the banister as Inspector Fournier's voice boomed from the foyer below.

"Your alibi for last night is thin, Marco. And let us not forget your professional interest in knowing which plants are safe to eat and which are not," Fournier said sharply, his words echoing off the walls.

He must more than suspect poison. It sounds as if he knows for sure. That meant both she and Marco could be suspects. Again.

"Inspector, my work with herbs and flowers is no secret, but it has nothing to do with DuPont's death!" Marco's defense was passionate yet controlled.

"Perhaps," Fournier mused, pacing back and forth on the checkerboard tiles. "But the fact remains, Mr. Bellamy, that you had both motive and opportunity. Once we know for sure what killed Monsieur DuPont, I imagine we'll also know for sure that you had means."

Alice felt a chill despite the warmth of the chateau. She hadn't thought about how Marco's business ventures could be misinterpreted, about how his passion for rare botanicals could become tangled in suspicion. Her gaze fell to the ornate patterns of the rug beneath her feet, its greens and blues reminding her of the hydrangea mystery they had pondered earlier. What had the Inspector meant about Marco having a motive, though? What reason could he possibly have had to want to DuPont dead? He'd been here for a shorter time than she had and she'd hadn't seen anything that would make her think there was unpleasantness between the two.

"Inspector, I respect your duty to investigate every angle," Marco continued, his tone earnest, "but I assure you, my interest in plants is purely for their culinary and aesthetic value and Monsieur DuPont and I had left our disagreements in the past. That was part of what this whole new venture was about."

Fournier paused, then said, "I hope for your sake that is true. For now, consider yourself a person of interest. Do not attempt to leave the country."

Alice drew back as footsteps approached the staircase. The conversation had ended, but the tension hung in the air like the aftertaste of a robust red wine, heavy and lingering. She waited for the sound of footsteps to fade before she dared move again.

Awareness of the scene's gravity settled in her chest. What past was Marco talking about? What motive had the Inspector been referring to? Hunger still nudged at her. With quiet steps, she resumed her descent, the mystery of the hydrangeas—and Marco's fate—spinning through her mind like the delicate tendrils of a vine searching for sunlight.

CHAPTER EIGHT

Alice stepped into the spacious, sunlit kitchen of Château DuPont and immediately sensed a storm brewing. The air was thick with the rich aromas of simmering herbs and garlic, but it was the bristling energy of Marco Bellamy, hunched over the cutting board, that captured her attention. His knife flashed angrily through a stalk of celery, his usually warm brown eyes clouded with frustration.

"Marco?" she ventured cautiously, her voice echoing slightly off the limestone walls. "Is everything alright?"

He paused, the tension in his broad shoulders betraying his agitation before he let out a long sigh. "I should never have come back here," he muttered, not meeting her gaze as he reached for a bunch of basil.

Her heart twinged with concern. "What do you mean? Back to Provence? Back to the Château? You were here before?"

"Years ago," Marco began, setting down the knife and finally looking up at her. The anger seemed to dissolve, leaving behind a trace of old pain. "Right after I graduated from the culinary institute, René— he hired me. I was to be the chef for some rather prestigious events right here." He tapped softly on the countertop with a closed fist.

Alice leaned against the worn wood. Marco was an amazing chef. She knew that from eating food he'd prepared. She hadn't asked a lot of questions about how he learned everything he knew, though, or what his path had been before it had crossed hers. Their conversations had mostly revolved around sustainable landscaping and the delicate balance of flavors in food and how that all intertwined. And solving murders, of course.

The only reason he knew about Scott was because of Scott's habit of turning up like the proverbial bad penny.

"I can see how that would be tempting to a new chef. Château DuPont has a reputation, of course," she said softly, encouraging him to continue. "It must have been a big opportunity for a recent graduate."

Marco gave a wry smile, picking up the knife once more but this time, his movements were slower, more deliberate. "Yes, it was. A huge opportunity. I leapt at it." He glanced out of the window to where the vineyards stretched out in well-ordered rows, their leaves whispering secrets in the light breeze. "But some opportunities come with unforeseen consequences."

Alice nodded. She knew there was more to the story, layers beneath the surface like the complex root systems of the plants she so loved. And like any good gardener, she understood the importance of patience, of waiting for the right moment to unearth the truth. She gave him space to continue.

Marco turned from the window, his brown eyes somber as he faced Alice. "René," he began, setting aside the knife and resting his broad palms on the edge of the cutting board, "he had a way of making you feel... small. As if your best was never quite enough. Even when I knew I had more knowledge than he did, he had a confidence in the way he expressed himself that made everyone else fall in line with his opinions."

Alice observed the tension in Marco's shoulders, the way his jaw clenched when he spoke of the past. She knew that feeling too well— the sharp sting of not being appreciated, of having your opinions discounted.

"He'd change menus at the last moment, demanding items for which I didn't have the right ingredients or that needed more time than I had, or dismiss my ideas for integrating herbs in ways that were unconventional. Forget my thoughts about edible flowers. He wouldn't even hear them. He would come in at the last minute and decide to add his own seasonings to dishes." A flash of the old fire returned to Marco's eyes, the passion that drew them into countless conversations about flavors and growth. "Eventually, I couldn't take it anymore. We argued. I quit. Or maybe I was fired. Or both. Regardless, our business relationship ended with a bitter taste, much like uncured olives."

"Yet here you are," Alice said, her gaze steady on him, encouraging him to connect the dots, to tell him how he'd ended up back at Château DuPont.

"Here I am," Marco confirmed, pushing a stray lock of dark hair behind his ear. "When René called me out of the blue to ask for help with food pairing for the wine competition, I was skeptical. But then— he mentioned you were going to be here, designing their gardens. And I thought, I don't know, maybe it was time to bury old grudges under new soil."

"So, you took the olive branch?" She couldn't resist a small smile, knowing Marco would appreciate the botanical metaphor.

"Something like that." He allowed himself a half-smile in return.

"We agreed to start fresh, no mention of the past. I thought maybe we could find some common ground over good food and fine wine."

"Common ground is a great place to grow from," Alice murmured, thinking of how plants needed the right environment to thrive—just like relationships. This would be the second time that her relationship with Marco was rooted in trouble and upheaval. What did that mean for them? If the roots of a plant rotted because of soil conditions, it often couldn't be saved.

"That's what I'd hoped," Marco affirmed, reaching for a sprig of rosemary and crushing it between his fingers, releasing its fragrance into the room. The simple act seemed to realign him with the present, with the kitchen of Château DuPont and the task at hand.

"Fresh start," Alice repeated, watching as Marco began to chop vegetables with renewed purpose.

Alice leaned against the doorframe, observing Marco as he slammed a pot onto the stovetop with more force than necessary. The kitchen, usually a sanctuary of aromatic herbs and simmering sauces, felt tense with unsaid words hanging in the air. "I wish you'd told me," she said, keeping her voice quiet and small.

His head drooped. "René had asked me to keep everything about our past secret. None of the staff now — Lilou, Sophie, Jean-Baptiste — had been here when I was here originally. He didn't want to give anyone a chance to stir up trouble between us."

"Why . . .," Alice stopped. She'd been about to ask why someone would want to stir up trouble, but she'd already sensed there were some unspoken currents running through the staff. Those glances between Lilou and Jean-Baptiste. They'd seemed innocent enough, but now their employer was dead. Was there more to those secret exchanges than it appeared?

"Inspector Fournier has his eyes on me," Marco said abruptly, without turning to face her. "He's dug up the old dirt between René and me. He thinks I might have had something to do with his murder, that I could have used some of the plants or herbs here to poison René."

His hands stilled on the wooden handle of the knife, and he looked at her then, brown eyes clouded with a mixture of anger and desperation. "I swear, Alice, I didn't have anything to do with René's death and I would never use food as a weapon. It's contrary to everything I believe in."

Alice pushed away from the doorframe and moved closer, her heart reaching out to him. She placed a reassuring hand on his broad shoulder, feeling the tension coiled in his muscles. "Marco, I believe you," she said, her voice steady and clear. "You're not capable of such an act."

She gave a wry smile, despite the gravity of the situation. "Besides, I'm apparently on the suspect list too. Seems my knowledge of poisonous plants is more than just professional curiosity to Fournier as well. He knew about me being a suspect in Italy, too."

Their gazes locked, a silent understanding passing between them. They were both outsiders in this lush estate of vines and secrets, bound by a love for nature's offerings and now, an accusation that threatened to uproot their lives.

"Then we're in this together," Marco stated, a resolute edge to his voice. "We'll clear our names. Again."

Alice nodded. "Together," she echoed, the word wrapping around them like a vine, strong and unyielding. "Let's dig up the truth and plant the seeds of justice once again."

Marco held out his hand, and they shook.

Their pact sealed, they turned back to the tasks before them – Marco to his lunch preparations, and Alice to the mystery that grew more tangled with each passing hour. But amidst the clatter of pots and the whiff of rosemary, hope blossomed anew, rooted in their shared trust and determination.

CHAPTER NINE

The clink of cutlery on porcelain was the only sound that broke the heavy silence hanging over the dinner table. Alice pushed her food around her plate, appetite waning in the shadow of the day's grim discovery. Across from her, Marco maintained a respectful quiet, his usual vibrant tales of life in various kitchens around the world left untold tonight.

Finally, Alice couldn't stand it anymore. Fournier had asked her not to discuss anything before the others were questioned, but he didn't say anything about afterwards. "What do you all think happened?"

It was like popping a balloon. The tension in the room went out with a whoosh.

"After dinner, René went out for a walk, as he often does." Lilou paused, then said, "Did. He often did. He liked to walk the perimeter, check the fences."

"Yes," Sophie said. "I saw him leave. Lilou was in the kitchen. I went in to make a cup of tea and we chatted."

"Did anyone see him after that?" Alice asked.

Around the table, everyone shook their heads.

"I went out to my cottage," Sophie said. Neither Sophie nor Jean-Baptiste had rooms in the actual château. Both had small bungalows, Sophie's near the wine cellars and Jean-Baptiste's near the garage.

"I turned in early," Jean-Baptiste said. "I didn't even hear Sophie return to her cottage."

"I don't think he ever came back after dinner," Lilou murmured. "When I went to make up his room this morning, the bed... it was already made." Her voice trailed off, and the collective sorrow tightened its grip. "I didn't think anything of it. I thought maybe his evening walk had been an excuse to meet up with a lady friend."

Alice's eyebrows shot up. "Did René have a lady friend?"

Lilou took a sip of wine. "I'm not certain. I thought perhaps he did. He'd been taking a little more care with his appearance lately and there were a few times when I couldn't find him and he was cagey about where he was. I thought maybe a romance he wasn't ready to make

48

public. Regardless, he didn't sleep in his bed last night."

So something had happened when René had gone out for his walk. Perhaps he'd gone to check on the hydrangeas as well and then fallen ill there. Alice's head dropped. How frightened he must have been. Poor man. He'd been all alone out there while Alice had drifted off with thoughts of those same flowers dancing in her head.

Sophie sat with her eyes cast down, fingers tracing the stem of her wine glass as if to draw strength from the very craft René had loved. After a moment, she cleared her throat and stood, glass held aloft.

"To René," she began, her tone steady despite the moisture threatening to spill from her eyes. "He was not just our employer, but my mentor. From soil composition to market trends, he gave me the opportunity to learn how to become an alchemist and to turn grapes into gold."

As she spoke, Jean-Baptiste caught Lilou's gaze, their eyes locking in an exchange thick with unspoken thoughts. Alice observed them, her curiosity piqued. What secrets were they keeping behind those shared glances?

"May his legacy continue through the vines he tended and the lives he touched." Sophie concluded, and the others raised their glasses in solemn agreement.

"Here's to René," they echoed, a chorus tinged with sadness.

The clink of cutlery against porcelain had slowed, and the last bites of the provincial ratatouille were taken in contemplative silence. Sophie set down her fork with a soft clatter and dabbed the corners of her mouth with a linen napkin before addressing the group.

"Despite this tragedy, Château DuPont's heart still beats," she announced, her voice carrying a new resolve that resonated in the dining room. "We will honor René by participating in the annual rosé competition as he wanted. The wine we've crafted, the one he named after his mother, is our tribute to him." She glanced around the table, her eyes reflecting the candlelight. "I spoke to his daughter in Canada. She'll be arriving soon, and she's adamant that we proceed with René's plans for the competition."

Alice, who had been tracing the veins of a vine leaf on her plate, looked up. The mention of René's daughter brought a fresh perspective to the unfolding events. "Will she take over running the château?" Alice asked.

Sophie shook her head gently, a wistful smile touching her lips as if she harbored fond memories of the absent heir. "No, I don't believe so. She's never shown any interest in winemaking or the business aspect of it. Although apparently, René didn't either until he was a bit older. I doubt she'd sell Château DuPont, though. It's been in their family for generations. It's more likely she'll appoint someone to manage it."

Marco nodded thoughtfully, swirling the last of his wine in his glass. The conversation seemed to breathe a small dose of hope into the air, dissipating some of the heaviness that had settled over them since René's untimely departure from life. "So we will continue with our plans for the tasting menu and the garden."

"Then there's much to be done," Lilou said, her voice quiet but determined. "We'll need to make sure everything is perfect for the heir's arrival—and for the competition."

There was a collective murmur of agreement. The future of Château DuPont hung in the balance, an enigma shrouded in the very vines that sprawled across the estate's lands. But one thing was certain—René's legacy would live on through the dedication of those he left behind.

Alice traced the rim of her wine glass as she pondered the group's subdued expressions. She cleared her throat gently, drawing their attention. "Was there anyone who might have disliked René? Someone who would benefit from his... absence?" Her voice was careful, tiptoeing around the weight of the question.

Lilou and Jean-Baptiste shared another glance that lingered a second too long, but neither spoke. Their silence hung in the air like mist over morning vines.

"Come on," Alice pressed, sensing the undercurrents of a deeper narrative. "What are you both thinking?"

Lilou folded her napkin, carefully smoothing it into a perfect rectangle. "Claire LeBlanc," she finally said, her words carrying a hint of reluctance. "Her land lies next to Château DuPont. The history between their families is..." She searched for the right word, "...complicated."

Jean-Baptiste nodded, his fingers drumming on the table. "Old feuds about property lines. Debates that have been aging as long as the wines in their cellars." He sighed, a sound that seemed to carry the burden of centuries.

"More recently," Lilou continued, "Claire had ambitions to expand her winery. But René... he resisted. Claimed the land she wanted to use belonged to him. Filed complaint after complaint, entangling her plans in bureaucracy until she abandoned them altogether."

French bureaucracy was notorious. It sounded like René had used that to his advantage. Alice absorbed this new information, considering the delicate ecosystem of relationships and rivalries that thrived alongside the grapes of Provence. Claire LeBlanc, she thought, a name now etched with suspicion in her mind. The pieces of the puzzle were slowly starting to take shape. Now, she had to see if she could organize them into a picture.

After dinner, without consultation, they all worked together to clear the table and clean the kitchen. Alice stacked the last of the clean dishes into the cupboard. The quiet clinks of porcelain and glass filled the spaces between hushed conversations as the group worked in a comfortable rhythm, clearing away the remnants of their subdued dinner.

Sophie, with the grace of someone who knew her way around both vines and hearts, retrieved a bottle from the cellar—a golden-hued dessert wine, still wearing the sheen of the underground coolness. "To brighter moments," she declared, uncorking the bottle with an expert twist. Her voice was light but carried an undercurrent of solemn remembrance. "This is a dessert wine I've been working on. I've only bottled a small amount. I hadn't even had René try it yet."

The pop of the cork seemed to break the somber spell that had settled over them. Glasses were lined up like sentinels on the counter, waiting to be filled with the liquid amber. As Sophie poured, the aromatic sweetness rose in the air, mingling with the lingering scents of herbs and roasted vegetables.

"René would have adored this," Lilou remarked, accepting a glass with a nod of appreciation. "Or he should have."

"Indeed," Jean-Baptiste agreed, his eyes softening at the rim of his own glass as he took a sip. The wine was lush with the promise of sun-drenched grapes, a testament to the skill hidden behind Sophie's modest smile.

Alice felt the mood shift gently, like the turning of the earth beneath her beloved plants. She accepted her own glass, the taste of the wine bright and complex on her tongue. It coaxed a small smile from her, despite the shadow that René's absence cast upon them all.

"Do you remember when René accidentally took a sip out of his spit cup instead of his wine glass at that tasting?" Lilou asked, a little smile on her lips.

Jean-Baptiste snorted. "Do I ever! The look on his face when he realized what he'd done!"

Sophie joined in. "And the story he told to make it seem like he'd done it on purpose!"

All three of them laughed.

"Shall we?" Marco asked Alice, tilting his head towards the French doors that led to the garden, as Jean-Baptiste started another anecdote. His brown eyes glinted with warmth in the low light of the chandelier.

"Let's," Alice replied. Outside, the moon bathed the garden in soft silver, making the leaves of the trees shimmer like whispers. They walked side by side, their footsteps a soft whisper on the gravel path. Around them, the world was alive with the night songs of cicadas and the rustle of the breeze.

Marco stopped by a bed of night-blooming jasmine, their delicate fragrance floating on the cool air. He turned to Alice, his gaze reflecting the glow of the moon above them. "This reminds me of Italy."

Alice knew what he meant. "There's a bit of magic here, too," she said, her voice barely sounding above the night's melody.

"Yes. In Italy, I thought the magic was from being on the Riviera. For a moment, I thought Provence was providing the magic here, too." He smiled. "I think the magic really comes from you, Alice. I think any place you are becomes special."

Their eyes met, and for a moment, the world seemed to pause. Marco reached out, his fingers brushing against hers, sending a current that felt like the first sprout of spring through her veins. He leaned in, and Alice closed her eyes, their lips meeting in a kiss that was as tender as the touch of dew on morning petals.

Above them, the moon witnessed the gentle unfurling of new love, its luminescent rays cradling them in a silent blessing. For now, the mystery of Château DuPont and its tangled vines could wait. In the embrace of the Provençal night, there was only the softness of Marco's lips and the sweet promise of blossoming affection.

CHAPTER TEN

Alice awoke to the gentle chirp of sparrows outside her window, the first rays of sunlight casting a soft glow across the vintage quilt on her bed. She stretched, her mind already turning over the details of René DuPont's untimely demise. Today, she would visit Château LeBlanc. The estate was renowned for its wine and—importantly—open to visitors only that day this week for tasting sessions, according to some Internet sleuthing she'd done the night before. She'd also let Owen know that the garden plans would be going forward. He'd been delighted, but had again asked her to be careful.

In the kitchen, Marco was already sipping espresso and flipping through a battered cookbook. He got up the second she walked in and gave her a good morning hug and a light kiss. "You look radiant today as usual, Alice. The way your hair catches the sunlight . . ." He gave a chef's kiss.

She laughed. "Flattery will get you everywhere, Marco."

"Is it still flattery when it's true?" He went over to the counter. "Café au lait and pain aux amandes?"

No wonder the room smelled amazing. She slid into the spot next to his at the table. "You're spoiling me again."

"Not possible." He turned to his task.

Alice turned the pages of the cookbook he'd been reading while she waited. It was in French and had the stained and battered pages of a set of recipes that had been used often and loved. "Where did you find this?"

"In the library," he said over his shoulder. "I thought I might find something that would honor the DuPont family history and René's mother, in particular. I think that's her cookbook."

Alice turned to the frontispiece and saw the name Jacqueline DuPont written in old-fashioned Palmer method script. "It would seem so. Anything interesting yet?"

"Yes! There's a recipe for rose petal jam here. I can't wait to get started on it. Is it okay to pick some of the roses from the garden?" He rubbed his hands together in excitement.

"Of course." Alice smiled. She loved his enthusiasm for his work.

"Anything else"

"Maybe. Certainly some ideas. Lots of old traditional Provencal recipes that could use some modern updates." He set the coffee and the pastry down in front of her. "You're not dressed for gardening this morning."

Alice looked down. She'd put on an outfit Daisy had given her. A sage green maxi t-shirt dress made from organic cotton and Tencel with a pair of ethically made slip-on sneakers. She had a short denim jacket to wear over it all in case it got chilly and, of course, a scarf. Maybe Jean-Baptiste would teach her how he tied his.

"I'm still figuring out exactly what I want to do out there," Alice said, after a bite of the pain aux amandes made her moan. "I was thinking I'd head over to Château LeBlanc today. I wanted to see what some of the surrounding gardens looked like before I made more plans for this one, and I thought maybe I'd be able to snoop around a bit while I was there to see if Claire LeBlanc could be somehow involved in René's death. Care to join me?"

Marco's brow furrowed ever so slightly. "Ah, I wish I could," he replied with a smile that didn't quite reach his eyes, "but I've got more research to do and some menus to plan."

A flicker of disappointment ran through Alice. She had hoped they would piece together the mystery side by side, as they had in Italy. His excuse, while plausible, left an unfamiliar knot in her stomach. It reminded her of something. She just wasn't sure what.

"Be sure to make a list of what herbs you'd like me to plant," she said.

"Oh, I will." The twinkle was back in Marco's eye. Maybe she'd been wrong about it disappearing.

She finished her breakfast and rinsed her plate and mug and went to find Jean-Baptiste to see if he could drive her. She found him in the winery, helping Sophie move some boxes. He seemed happy to change chores.

The drive to Château LeBlanc was smooth, Jean-Baptiste maneuvering the car through turns in a way that told Alice he'd driven these road before. As they pulled up the gravel driveway, flanked by rows of meticulously pruned vines, Alice's focus sharpened. Each detail, from the dew on the grape leaves to the subtle gradations of soil, was a potential clue.

"Here we are, Mademoiselle Bloom," Jean-Baptiste announced as he maneuvered the car smoothly into a secluded corner of the parking area, shaded by an overhanging canopy of oak branches. He killed the engine and turned to Alice with a smile.

"I'll be right here when you're done in there," he assured her, nodding toward the Château's distant spires.

"You don't mind waiting?" Alice asked. "I could call you when I'm ready to go back to the château."

Jean-Baptiste gave one of those elegant Gallic shrugs. "Waiting is part of the job description for us drivers."

"Thanks, Jean-Baptiste," Alice said, giving him a grateful look. She stepped out of the car, ready to immerse herself in the world of wine and whispers. Visitor parking was around a quarter mile from the winery itself and largely out of sight of the actual château. That suited her fine as she knelt to feel the soil. It was loose and crumbly, a little coarse because of the small stones in it. She sniffed at it and got a slightly mineral aroma. She took out a little vial and took a sample of it to test back at the lab with Sophie, but she would be surprised if it was either very alkaline or acidic. It seemed well-balanced and ideal for the grapes growing there.

"Gonna take a taste of it, ma fleur?" A voice called.

She bowed her head for a second before standing up. "Scott?" Yep. There he was. His tall, lanky frame was unmistakable, even from a distance. It used to make her heart beat faster. Now, it mainly annoyed her. Scott was selfish and self-involved. It didn't seem fair that it was all bound up in a handsome package. "What are you doing here?"

He walked over and took her hand to help her step back onto the gravel of the parking lot. "I'm doing a little detective work. Seems like LeBlanc has a couple of greenhouses she won't let anyone in. I'm wondering if she's hiding that rare orchid I've been chasing. Thought I'd pretend to be here for a tour and wine tasting and poke around a bit. You?"

Well, that was awfully similar to what Alice herself was doing here. "I wanted to see what other nearby wineries had done with their grounds and --" Her words trailed off. Could she trust Scott? She knew she couldn't trust him with her heart, but with something like this maybe she could. He'd been a huge help back in Italy.

"Spit it out, Alice."

She bristled, but at least he hadn't called her his flower again. "The LeBlanc and DuPont families were apparently at odds and had been for a while. I thought I'd poke around a bit, too. Maybe see if Claire could have had anything to do with what happened to René."

Scott clapped his hands. "Excellent. We're going undercover! I love that for us."

Alice rolled her eyes. "There is no 'us,' Scott."

"Sure there is." He paused. "Maybe a different us than there was a few years ago. That's my fault. I admit that. But that doesn't mean everything we had in common has disappeared."

He was right. Many of the things that had brought them together were still there. "What do you suggest as our cover?"

"How about we play newlyweds? Tourists love these places. It'll give us cover while we investigate." He grinned.

Alice hesitated, memories of their shared passion for botany—and the subsequent heartache—flashing through her mind. Yet the ruse had merit. It would let them whisper to each other as they noted things without anyone wanting to know what they were talking about. With a reluctant nod, she agreed. "Newlyweds it is, then," she conceded, mustering a smile, though the role felt like a mask she wasn't sure she wanted to wear again.

He offered her his arm, and she took it. Then together they stepped onto the pathway that led to Château LeBlanc, embarking on a charade amidst the vines.

The grounds of Château LeBlanc unfurled before them like a well-tended secret, rows of vines marching in disciplined lines to the horizon. In front of them was a straight path that led directly to the courtyard. Along the way, several other paths intersected with the main path at right angles, and a lovely fountain burbled in the spot where they came together. Everything was controlled and symmetrical. It was classy and elegant and exactly what René hadn't wanted for the gardens at his winery. Alice understood why. There was a message beneath the beauty that had to do with people having dominion over nature rather than living in harmony with it. She appreciated its beauty, but it wasn't what she wanted to create.

"Look there," Alice whispered to Scott, pointing discreetly at a bed of calla lilies nestled among the foliage. "Beautiful, but deadly if you know what you're doing. Calla lilies contain calcium oxalate crystals, sharp on a microscopic level. If ingested, they can cause severe burning and irritation."

Scott raised his eyebrows. "And those?" he asked, nodding toward the dark green needles of a yew shrub. "I've heard those can be nasty."

"Taxus baccata, yew," Alice replied, her eyes narrowing as she regarded the plant. There was more than a little of it at Château DuPont as well. "Every part of it is toxic, especially the seeds."

They continued their stroll, the sun warm on their backs, the air rich with the scent of earth and ripening grapes.

"LeBlanc had easy access to both plants," she mused aloud. "If DuPont was poisoned and that's definitely the vibe I'm getting from Fournier, she could have cooked up all kinds of things that would do the trick without ever leaving her property, especially if she has a lab like Sophie's."

"Let's not jump to conclusions," Scott cautioned, though his gaze remained thoughtful. "But it's certainly a piece of the puzzle worth considering."

Alice nodded, filing away the information in her mental catalogue of clues. As she walked, the shadow of René DuPont seemed to whisper through the leaves, urging her to look closer, dig deeper, and uncover the truth.

If she hadn't been looking so closely, she likely would have missed the path hidden behind the yew hedges. As it was, she glimpsed only a little bit of the gray gravel through the dark green needles and red berries. "Scott," she whispered, pulling him to a stop.

He stepped closer to her so their chests nearly touched. "What?" He looked down at her, then brushed a lock of hair behind her ear. "Damn, I've missed the way your hair glows in the sun. Like a river of red and gold."

She took a step away from him. "Scott, no."

"Fine." He sighed. "Then what, Alice?"

With a nod of her head, she indicated where the path was. "There's something that way. Do you think that's where your secret greenhouse could be?"

Looking over in the direction she'd indicated, he smiled. "It's certainly worth checking out. Good catch. You always did have sharp eyes."

"Thanks." She took his arm again, and they walked along the paths, looking for a route in the direction they wanted to go.

They found it, eventually, a narrow place where the grass had been flattened perhaps by wheelbarrows being pushed on it. They followed it up and over a small hill to find the greenhouse, set like a crystal palace against the backdrop of Château LeBlanc's sprawling vineyards. Patches of sunlight played hide and seek through the glass panes, casting a patterned glow on the earthy floor within. They slipped inside, the humidity wrapping around them like a warm cloak.

"Look for Cypripedium kentuckiense ," Scott whispered, his eyes scanning the vibrant sprawl of greenery.

"Kentucky Ladyslipper?" Alice surveyed the rows of orchids with an expert eye but found no sign of the rare pale yellow bloom. Her gaze lingered on the dew-speckled petals and lush foliage, feeling a twinge of disappointment for him.

"It's one part of the hybrid I've heard about." He stepped into another row to get a better look at the plants there.

Suddenly, the sound of approaching footsteps snapped her back to reality. A gardener, clad in overalls with a trowel holstered like a weapon, rounded the corner and frowned at the sight of them.

"Vous ne devriez pas être ici," he said sternly, his stance suggesting they were more than just unwelcome guests.

Before Alice could conjure up an excuse, Scott stepped forward, his arm sliding around her waist and pulling her close against him. With no warning, he pressed his lips to hers—a brief, albeit convincing, kiss that left her cheeks flushed with shock.

"Nous sommes désolés," Scott said smoothly, once he pulled away. "We're newlyweds, just looking for a little...privacy."

The gardener's face softened into a reluctant smile, and with a shake of his head, he waved them off, muttering about young love.

Alice's heart was still racing from the unexpected kiss as they headed to the wine tasting room, a cavernous space filled with the clinking of glasses and murmur of conversations.

They walked up to an empty spot at the long bar, and an elegant woman in her mid-thirties came over to them with a smile. "Bonjour, my name is Claire. Welcome to Château LeBlanc. What brings you to Provence?"

Alice's eyes widened. It was the proprietress herself. "I guess it's obvious we're tourists."

LeBlanc shrugged as only the French can. "I have a discerning eye."

Scott pulled Alice tight against him. "We're on a little honeymoon jaunt."

She fought the urge to squirm away from him despite how natural it felt to have his arm around her, a little too much like old times. It was an act, she reminded herself. Nothing more. "We were hoping to learn more about your wines and your château."

"Certainly." LeBlanc poured two small samples of wine. "This is a lovely, refreshing rosé. The color is a delicate, pale salmon hue - a hallmark of high-quality Provençal rosés, as this one is."

"Cheers, my dear wife," Scott quipped, raising his glass with a wink.

She played along, clinked her glass against his, and drank her small sample, appreciating its notes of summer berries.

The second they set their glasses down, LeBlanc poured another sample. "This is from last year's harvest. You'll note the delicate aromas of fresh red berries, maybe some strawberry and raspberry, along with a subtle floral note and a hint of citrus zest."

Alice and Scott drank again. And so it went through several more samples. Alice swayed a little as she drank the last one.

"Easy there, honey bunch." Scott caught hold of her arm to steady her.

Claire smiled. "We have just one more sample, a little experiment we're making with dessert wine."

Alice tasted it and then remembered the wine that Sophie had brought out for them the night before. This was similar. "We hear Château DuPont is experimenting with some similar wines. Have you tasted their new rosé?"

Claire's mouth twisted. "Oh, yes. The one Monsieur DuPont is naming after his mother."

"Yes," Alice said. "That's the one. What do you think of it?"

Claire leaned forward, resting her elbows on the long polished wood counter. "I think that if René had had more time and respect for his mother when she was alive, he wouldn't have needed to hire outside help to make his wines."

Scott shook his head. "He wasn't good to his mother? I'm not sure there's much that speaks more poorly of a man."

Claire stood and pointed at him. "Very true. I learned my trade at the knees of my parents. Winemaking was their life and now it's mine. I suppose I shouldn't speak ill of the dead, but René was just a dilettante. Not a bad businessman, though."

"How so?" Alice asked, genuinely curious.

"He knew when something was too much for him to handle." Claire picked up a wineglass and polished it with a white cotton rag. "He knew when to ask for help."

Alice blinked a few times, trying to get everything to seem less woozy. "Did he ask you for help?"

Claire set the glass down with a quiet clink. "Yes. He did. I suppose there's no reason not to talk about it now. We were keeping it under wraps. We were in negotiations to merge our operations. After years of our families feuding, we were looking to cooperate. He was better at the business end of things than I am. I'm better at making wine."

"So there were no disputes between you?" Alice asked, trying hard not to slur her words.

Claire laughed. "There certainly used to be. There's an area I

59

wanted to expand into with new varietals. He claimed it was his land, and we had quite the go-round about it. Negotiating over that was actually how we got the idea to merge. We realized that together we would be greater than the sum of our parts."

"What happens now that he's dead?" Scott asked.

"We'll have to see." Claire sighed. "I'll approach his daughter when things settle."

Alice nodded. "So you had no reason to murder him. You would be better off if he stayed alive."

Claire's eyes blazed. "Excuse me! What did you just say? Did you actually accuse me of murdering René DuPont?"

Alice's cheeks got hot when she realized she'd voiced her thoughts out loud. "Oh, no. So sorry. Just thinking out loud."

LeBlanc's eyes narrowed into icy slits. "Perhaps you would think more clearly outside my property," LeBlanc suggested, gesturing toward the exit with a flick of her wrist.

Scott pulled Alice toward the exit. Her mind buzzed with more than just the effects of the wine. Could LeBlanc be René's secret lady friend? Were they talking about merging more than their businesses and land? She planted her feet and turned to face Claire. "Mademoiselle LeBlanc, were you having an affair with René DuPont?"

LeBlanc's expression remained unreadable, but the slightest tightening of her jaw hinted at ripples beneath the calm surface. Without a word, she turned on her heel and disappeared into the back room.

"Very subtle, Bloom. You never could hold your liquor worth a damn," Scott observed as he guided Alice back to the parking lot. The golden hue of the afternoon sun bathed the vineyards in a warm glow. "Quite the adventure we're having."

"More like a misadventure," Alice corrected with a small smile, her cheeks still flushed from the wine, the awkwardness of their staged intimacy, and the confrontation with LeBlanc.

Jean-Baptiste spotted them from his position leaning against the sleek black car, his posture ever patient. He pushed off from the vehicle and opened the passenger door as they approached.

"Miss Bloom," he greeted her, a knowing look in his eyes as if he could sense the undercurrents of the day without a word being said.

"Thank you, Jean-Baptiste," Alice replied, climbing into the backseat with a grateful nod. "Good-bye, Scott. Good luck finding your Ladyslipper."

Jean-Baptiste shut the door and Alice settled into the plush leather, feeling the weight of her eyelids growing heavier with each passing second. Day drinking was not in her skill set.

"Back to Château DuPont then?" Jean-Baptiste asked, his voice steady if a little amused as he started the engine.

"Please," she murmured, her body sinking further into the comfort of the seat.

The car purred to life, gliding forward with a smoothness that seemed to rock Alice gently. As the vehicle wove through the winding roads, the rhythmic hum of the tires on gravel became a lullaby.

Outside, rows upon rows of grapevines passed by in a blur of green and brown. The scents of earth and growing things filled the car, mingling with the faint aroma of the wine that still clung to Alice's breath.

Alice's breathing evened out, the events of the day—the sneaking into the greenhouse, the unexpected kiss, the wine that loosened her tongue—all drifted away as slumber claimed her.

CHAPTER ELEVEN

Alice's head shot up as the car came to a stop.

"We're here, Alice," Jean-Baptiste said.

She surreptitiously checked her chin for drool as Jean-Baptiste came around to open the door for her. "Thank you, Jean-Baptiste." She felt a little steadier on her feet than she had as they'd left Château LeBlanc, but also terribly thirsty.

Marco came out of the kitchen, drying his hands on a dish towel. "You're back! I didn't realize you'd be gone quite so long. You missed lunch."

Alice couldn't help but smile. Of course the first thing Marco would be worried about was whether or not she had eaten. Being involved with a chef definitely had its perks. "I don't suppose there's anything I could have to eat now. I, uh, might be a little tipsy still."

Jean-Baptiste snorted and then schooled his face into something more nonchalant when she turned. "Monsieur Thorne mentioned that they made quite generous pours in the LeBlanc tasting room."

"Monsieur Thorne?" Marco said. "Scott was there?"

The name dropped between them like a lead weight, and Alice watched as Marco's jaw tensed. She understood his displeasure; Scott's unexpected presence had unsettled her, too. On the other hand, he had come in quite handy as her cover while investigating Claire LeBlanc.

"Let's not talk about him," she replied quickly, eager to steer away from the subject. "I really could use something to eat."

"Come on then." Marco draped an arm around her shoulders, leading her to the sanctuary of the kitchen as Jean-Baptiste drove the car off toward the garage behind them.

The room welcomed her with its familiar aromas of herbs and freshly baked bread. Marco went straight to work, deft hands assembling a charcuterie board with an array of cheeses, meats, and little bowls of olives and nuts. Alice perched on a stool by the counter, watching him move. It was like watching a dancer. There was a confidence to how he worked in the kitchen. She didn't mind watching the play of muscles in his forearms and he sliced and cubed items for the board, either.

As he placed the board in front of her, she bit into a wedge of cheese, its creaminess a comfort. "Mmmmm."

"So what did you learn at Château LeBlanc?" Marco asked, taking a seat next to her and helping himself to a fig wrapped in prosciutto.

"I learned that Claire LeBlanc has access to a number of poisonous plants she could have used to kill René. We saw yew and calla lily."

"I imagine you'd be hard pressed to find many châteaus that don't have poisonous plants on their grounds," Marco observed.

Fair point. There was plenty of yew right here at Château DuPont, too. Calla lily as well. "She definitely wasn't a fan of René as a winemaker, but it seemed like the two of them were healing old rifts and talking about going into business together. She said he had good business sense."

"How did you bring him up?" Marco asked.

Alice ate another wedge of cheese. "She served us a dessert wine and I asked if she had tried any of Château DuPont's wines. It didn't take much more than that to get her going. Until I started thinking out loud about murder. My whisper may have not have been as whispery as I thought it was."

Marco chuckled. "Ah. The drunk whisper. Never as quiet as people think it is."

"Tipsy," Alice corrected, pointing a finger at him. "Not drunk."

"Fine," Marco said, a smile tugging at the corner of his mouth. "Tipsy."

Alice traced the edge of an artisanal cracker with her finger, her thoughts knitting together a theory that seemed to grow thorns the deeper she delved. "We only have her word about the business deal between her and René. Or she might want to make the deal with René's daughter and take over running both wineries with René out of the way. She definitely didn't think much of his winemaking knowledge. Considering how close LeBlanc's property is to DuPont's vineyard," she mused aloud, "it would've been easy for Claire to slip in unnoticed, though. It's not like there's a lot of security out here." Her eyes met Marco's, searching for a flicker of agreement.

She didn't get one.

"You're letting your imagination run wild because of a few plants and some old arguments," he said, brushing crumbs from the counter with a sweep of his hand. "I can't see Claire LeBlanc as a murderer."

Alice frowned at his dismissal, the pieces of her puzzle refusing to align. "And why not?" she pressed. "What do you know about her?"

"Let's just say," Marco began, but caught himself, shaking his head.

"Never mind. It's not important right now."

A wrinkle formed between Alice's brows, her curiosity piqued by his evasion. But before she could probe further, Marco shifted gears, his tone taking on an edge of something she couldn't quite place. "So what was Scott doing at Château LeBlanc? Did he know you were going to be there?"

Alice shook her head. "I'm not sure how he would have known. It was a coincidence. He's still on the hunt for that Kentucky Ladyslipper that he thinks someone has around here." She frowned. "Not the Ladyslipper exactly, but some hybrid it's part of.

"Or so he says," Marco muttered.

"It does feel like more than a coincidence that he keeps turning up, but it doesn't matter. Scott is history," she stated firmly, though her thoughts briefly betrayed her, fluttering to how natural it had felt to be close to him. She focused back on Marco, determined to keep the conversation grounded in the here and now. "There's nothing between Scott and me," she said, her voice definite although her fingers trembled a against the cool glass of water Marco had poured for her. "After what happened in Morocco, forgiveness isn't in the cards." Scott had ditched her to chase after a rumor about an orchid. He'd left her alone in a foreign country. She'd gone home only to find tragedy there. It had been a watershed moment in her life.

She popped an olive into her mouth, savoring the briny taste that helped anchor her to the present moment. Yet, despite her words, a rogue memory slipped through the cracks of her resolve. She saw herself back in the humid embrace of the greenhouse, the air fragrant with the scent of earth and blossoming plants. Scott's lips had found hers with an unexpected gentleness, the memory so vivid she could almost feel the brush of his mouth against her skin.

Her heart fluttered, an involuntary response to the recollection of how he had once made her feel so effortlessly lifted from reality, as if they were the only two people in the world. It was a dance of romance and adventure, his hands guiding her through the labyrinth of exotic plants, each one a testament to their shared passion for the beauty and mystery of flora. Except it had turned out that Scott's passion wasn't for beauty or mystery. It was for money.

"Scott was a lifetime ago," Alice added, breaking the spell of her own thoughts. She reached for a slice of cured meat, the savory flavor another reminder that the past was just that—the past. "And I've moved on."

"But has he?" Marco asked. "It seems like he's always trying to find a way back into your good graces."

"That's his problem, not mine." The tightness in Alice's chest eased as she focused on the textures and tastes of the charcuterie board Marco had prepared, the simple pleasure of good food grounding her. She couldn't help but feel there was something he wasn't telling her, something more than having known René in the past. She glanced at him, appreciative of his concern but determined to keep her heart guarded.

She never wanted it to be broken again.

CHAPTER TWELVE

Alice's phone buzzed against the wooden surface of her desk the next morning. She looked away from the list of plants to purchase she'd been making. She hoped she could buy some of them today. She'd talk to the local nursery while she was there, too, to see if they knew anyone who could do some of the bigger jobs like taking out yew and making some new paths that weren't so symmetrical and stiff. The screen flashed Scott's name, an intrusion she wasn't prepared for so early in the morning.

"Meet me for coffee?" his voice came through, casual yet insistent.

"I'm rather busy with the garden plans, Scott," Alice replied. She pushed away from the desk, though.

"Heard some chatter about René that might interest you," he said, a lilt in his tone that Alice knew all too well.

"Can't you just tell me now?" She pressed the phone to her cheek, flicking through notes on her desk.

"Where's the fun in that?" Scott countered.

With a sigh, she acquiesced. Information, especially regarding René, was too crucial to ignore. She needed to go into town to purchase plants anyway. "Fine. Where?"

"Le Petit Café on Rue des Lilas. You'll love it."

She rolled her eyes. The café wasn't the point. "All right, see you soon." She hung up, her curiosity piqued despite herself, and went to find Jean-Baptiste.

"Do you have time to take me into town? I need to go to the nursery to order some plants and, um, meet someone for a coffee." She found herself blushing.

"Bien sûr, Mademoiselle Alice. When would you like to leave?"

She glanced at her watch. "Sooner rather than later."

"I'm ready when you are."

"Fantastic! Let me just go get my bag."

Jean-Baptiste was waiting by the car when she came downstairs. The drive into town was silent, punctuated only by the gentle hum of the engine and the passing scenery of vineyards blurring into green waves.

They stopped first at the nursery and with Jean-Baptiste's help to get past the language barrier, she managed to order much of what she wanted to plant in the next few days. Delivery wouldn't be until the next day, but that was fine. She'd need the afternoon and more to get the beds ready for planting. The nursery gave her some names of people who might be able to help with the some of her plans as well.

"Merci, Jean-Baptiste," Alice murmured as they pulled up to the sidewalk café. He nodded, a ghost of a smile on his lips, and parked the car under a canopy of plane trees.

She approached the café. Scott was right. She did love it. It was adorable. There were wrought iron chairs and mosaic tabletops and plants. It was nestled comfortably on the corner, inviting passersby with the rich scent of roasted coffee beans and the soft melody of a distant accordion.

Scott was there, tall and lanky, his blond hair catching the sunlight like strands of gold. He waved her over, a cup already in hand. She slipped into the chair opposite him, the ironwork cool against her back.

"I didn't think café culture was your thing," Alice remarked, eyeing the steaming espresso before him.

"There's more to life than orchids and adventure, Alice," he said. A waiter came over and set a cup in front of Alice. "I took the liberty of ordering for you."

She took a cautious sip, the robust flavor pleasantly surprising her. "Not bad," she conceded.

"Thought you'd approve." Scott leaned back, studying her with those piercing blue eyes.

Alice glanced around, taking in the patrons chatting leisurely, the waitstaff moving with efficient grace, the sun-dappled cobblestones. She couldn't remember the last time she had simply sat down to enjoy a place without thoughts of soil pH or the best angle for a trellis intruding.

"Nice spot," she admitted, the corners of her mouth twitching upwards.

"Sometimes, you've got to slow down, Alice. Take in the little things," he suggested, his gaze following a pigeon pecking at crumbs nearby.

"That's quite a different tune than you used to sing," she replied, but her eyes lingered on a bee hovering around a pot of geraniums, its dance a reminder of nature's effortless beauty amidst the small city's bustle.

Scott reached across the table enclosing Alice's hand in a tentative grasp. "You know," he said, his voice low and earnest, "we could both use a lesson in slowing down. Smelling the roses, as it were."

The unexpected warmth of his touch sent a ripple of surprise up her arm. Alice looked down at their intertwined fingers, noting how sun had weathered his skin since Morocco, when his pursuit of a legendary orchid had left her abandoned among the dunes.

As if reading her mind, he said, "I'm not the man who chased that foolish dream anymore," Scott continued, his thumb stroking the back of her hand. "I've come to realize success means nothing if you're alone at the finish line."

Alice felt a flutter in her chest, a sensation she hadn't expected. She withdrew her hand, folding it safely in her lap beneath the table. The bee from before now buzzed around a sugar packet someone had left behind. .

"Let's talk about René," she prompted, steering the conversation back to safer territory. "What have you heard?"

Scott hesitated, the hint of a frown crossing his features before he masked it with a smile. He leaned forward, the earnestness in his eyes replaced by something more else.

"Word is..." he began, lowering his voice as though the flowers themselves might be eavesdropping. "René made a few enemies. One of them is Geoffrey Lambert. He's a sommelier with quite the chip on his shoulder—seems he believes René's critical reviews of his work did some lasting damage to his career."

Alice arched an eyebrow, her interest piqued. "Where can I find this Lambert?"

Scott nodded toward the window, where a colorful poster flapped gently in the breeze. It advertised a local wine fest, bold letters proclaiming 'Tomorrow! Indulge in the region's finest!' Beneath it, smaller print listed names of participants. She frowned. Château DuPont wasn't on the list.

"Right there," Scott pointed out one particular name. "Geoffrey Lambert will be guiding attendees in a wine tasting adventure."

"Thanks," Alice said, her tone all business as she mentally filed away the information. She took a sip of her coffee, letting the rich aroma ground her thoughts back into focus.

"What do you say we go to that wine fest together? As newlyweds again?" He smiled. "I thought we had some good moments over at Château LeBlanc."

Alice set her cup down with a clink, her gaze meeting his squarely. He was talking about the greenhouse kiss. She could tell by that smirk on his face. She wouldn't lie and say it wasn't a good kiss, but there was a whole lot more to a relationship than successful lip locks. "Absolutely not, Scott." There was no room for misinterpretation in her voice.

With that, she stood up, leaving the charming café and its temptations behind. Jean-Baptiste was waiting by the car, ready to whisk her back to Château DuPont. As they drove off, Jean-Baptiste glanced at her through the rearview mirror.

"Monsieur Thorne has been around quite a bit, n'est ce pas?" he asked, a note of curiosity threading through his words. "He is an old friend?"

"Pretty much," Alice replied, looking out the window and not wanting to go into too much detail. The rolling vineyards passed by in a blur of green and gold. Had Scott really changed? Or was this another ploy? "I'm sure he'll be moving on soon. He never stays in one place for too long."

Back at the château, Alice went up to her room to change into her gardening clothes. Straw hat firmly planted on her head, Alice knelt by the hydrangeas. They were getting worse., looking more bedraggled by the day. Was it only a coincidence that she'd found René's body among themCould there be any connection between the hydrangeas and his death? She reached for her phone nestled in the pocket of her gardening apron, dialed Professor Greenway's number, and waited as the cool breeze rustled the leaves around her.

"Professor Greenway, it's Alice Bloom again," she said, once the line connected. "I've got some questions about the hydrangeas situation I told you about before..

"Ah, my dear Alice," came the warm, knowing voice over the line. "Tell me more."

Alice described the condition of the plants in detail, her eyes scanning the expanse of the garden. "There's more, though," she added hesitantly. "René DuPont... he's been murdered. I was the one who found him. He was in the hydrangeas. I can't help but wonder if there's a connection with the state of the garden. What do you think?"

There was a brief silence on the other end, and Alice could picture Professor Greenway, glasses perched on the bridge of her nose, pondering the question. "Let's think this through. One way the soil could have become too acidic is by the application of an ammonium nitrate fertilizer. Those fertilizers can be quite toxic to humans if it's ingested or inhaled."

Alice sat back on her heels, looking at the hydrangeas with pity.

"So if someone applied ammonium nitrate fertilizer to the hydrangeas, maybe they could have applied it to René as well."

"It's possible. But who would have done such a thing?" the professor finally asked, her tone sharpening with curiosity.

"I'm trying to figure that out." Alice picked a yellowed leaf off the hydrangeas. "I don't think the fertilizer explains everything about these hydrangeas."

"Putting one thing on a plant doesn't stop anyone from putting something else on it," Professor Greenway mused. "More than one substance would explain more than one symptom."

"Good point!" She'd been thinking too narrowly. She tapped her index finger against her lips as she thought. "What could cause the other symptoms?"

"Salt would be the easiest thing to get and to apply," Professor Greenway said. "Do you have a salinity meter?"

"I do! I tucked it in my bag when I packed. I'll check that!" Alice said goodbye and ran up to her room to get the meter. She'd taken the time to calibrate before she'd left home. Back down at the hydrangeas, she turned the meter on and inserted it into the soil. Her eyes grew wide at the reading. More than 5 decisiemens per meter or dS/m. Anything over 4 would be a problem. She took another reading on the other side of the hydrangeas and got the same result.

Out of curiosity, she went over to the bed where she planned to put in some of the plants she'd purchased that morning. Less than 1 dS/m. No way could the two patches of soil so close together be that different unless someone had done something to the hydrangeas deliberately. She'd already suspected that, but now it was confirmed. It also helped to know what had been done although trying to change the soil that had been tampered with could be time-consuming and expensive.

She gathered her tools and headed for the area she'd designated for edible flower garden. She'd want to get those plants into the ground quickly once they arrived. She pressed the cool metal of the garden spade into the earth, turning over the loamy soil as she contemplated her next move. The sun played peekaboo through the leaves, casting dappled shadows over her work. Her fingers delved into the rich, dark soil, parting it gently to make room for the new plantings.

Her movements were rhythmic and practiced, a dance between gardener and nature. Then, amidst the begonias and vincas and sweet alyssum, she halted, her breath catching in her throat. There, nestled inconspicuously among the other plants were the delicate, fern-like fronds of hemlock.

"Conium maculatum," she whispered, the Latin name rolling off her tongue. The discovery sent a shiver down her spine. Could this toxic intruder, hidden in plain sight, have been the instrument of René's demise?

Hemlock was extremely toxic, every bit of it. It worked quickly, and every bit of it was deadly. You didn't even have to ingest it. It could be inhaled or absorbed through the skin. Or it could be some kind of mistake. Hemlock was often confused with Queen Anne's lace, yarrow, wild fennel, and even elderflower.

She sat back on her heels, the implications of her find blooming like the very flowers she tended. If hemlock had crept into the Château's gardens, what else might be lurking, veiled beneath the surface? With care, she extracted the plant, contemplating its sinister potential.

"René," she said softly, envisioning the master vintner with his robust laugh and commanding presence, now silenced forever. Had someone used his garden's own bounty to end his life? The question hung heavily in the air, mixing with the scent of thyme and rosemary.

Alice's fingers sifted through the soil, her mind whirling with thoughts as potent as the venomous plant she had just unearthed. With each overturned clod of earth, her concerns deepened, branching out like the roots of the perennials she tended to. What if the presence of hemlock wasn't an accident? What if it had been deliberately planted with someone waiting to use it when the time was right? Security at the Château wasn't exactly tight. Someone could have easily snuck in both to plant the hemlock and to use it.

Could there be more hemlock in the garden? She wiped a bead of sweat from her brow. The afternoon sun cast long shadows across the Château, and in that moment, the beauty of the estate seemed to mask a darker narrative. Alice's role had shifted subtly from gardener to detective, her trowel now a tool for excavation in more ways than one.

The whisper of leaves seemed to echo her thoughts, a rustling susurration that spoke of secrets and stories woven into the very landscape. The gardens now felt like chapters in a botanical thriller, each plant a potential character with motives hidden beneath its foliage.

With a gentle touch, she checked the surrounding plants, her eyes sharp for any sign of unnatural additions. She looked for foxglove with its stunning blooms and toxic heart, the oleander's sweet scent belying its lethal sap and arum lily.

As dusk began to paint the sky in hues of pink and lavender, Alice realized she hadn't thought about Scott for hours. Focused on her passion, she felt a sense of contentment. Maybe Scott had changed, but she had changed, too. She wasn't the same woman he'd left in Morocco. She went upstairs to clean up and get ready for what she was sure would be another delicious dinner.

***

The dining room of Château DuPont was alive with the clinking of cutlery and the low murmur of congenial conversation. At the head of the long, oak table, Marco presented his latest culinary creation with a flourish. The rich aroma of a cassoulet, a tapestry of meats and beans seasoned with herbs Alice could identify by scent alone, filled the room.

"Nothing warms the heart like a traditional cassoulet," Marco said with a smile, serving generous portions onto each plate.

Sophie, her dark eyes reflecting the candlelight, uncorked a bottle and poured a deep red cabernet franc into everyone's glass. "This will bring out the earthiness of the beans and complement the savory flavors," she explained.

As they tasted the pairing, Marco nodded in agreement. "Sophie, you've outdone yourself. This wine is the perfect companion to the heartiness of the dish."

"Thank you, Marco. It's all about finding the right balance," Sophie replied, the corners of her eyes crinkling with pleasure.

Amidst the shared appreciation of the meal, Alice leaned back in her chair, allowing the conversation to wash over her. She swirled the wine in her glass, watching as it caught the light, thinking of the days ahead.

"Speaking of wine pairings," Alice interjected during a lull, "there's a wine fest in town tomorrow. Anyone interested in going?"

Lilou set down her fork. "I'll have to pass. There's business to attend to here at the château."

"I've asked Lilou to step up into a more managerial role," Sophie said. "I'm afraid René left a bit of a jumble on his desk. She's got a lot to sort through, but I was already planning on attending the wine fest. I want to check out the competition... and perhaps look for opportunities. René's daughter may not keep me on."

"Count me in," Marco chimed, his eyes meeting Alice's. "It would be interesting to see what the local vintners are doing these days and what pairings they're making."

Jean-Baptiste, who had been quietly enjoying his meal, spoke up from the end of the table. "I'll drive you all. It's settled then."

Alice nodded, relieved by their responses. She didn't mention her suspicions about Geoffrey Lambert or tell anyone about the hemlock she'd found. For now, it was enough to enjoy the company, the food, and the promise of tomorrow's exploration.

CHAPTER THIRTEEN

The next morning, Alice felt the kind of enthusiasm usually reserved for children looking a pile of wrapped presents on a birthday morning as a delivery truck, painted in a vibrant shade of green that seemed to echo the lushness of its cargo, backed up into the driveway of Château DuPont, its rear doors nearly bursting open to reveal rows upon rows of potted plants.

"Here they are," Alice said, unable to keep the excitement from her voice as she approached the vehicle.

Marco walked up beside her, his gaze taking in the array of greenery. "You've got quite the selection here, Alice."

With care, they began to unload the plants, setting them gently onto the gravel path. Each pot contained a world of potential—verdant leaves waiting to unfurl under the Provence sun, roots eager to stretch into rich soil. Marco picked up a fragrant basil and inhaled deeply, the scent mingling with the warm notes of earth still clinging to his hands.

"Where do you think this one should go?" he asked, looking over at Alice whose fingers were already caressing the feathery fronds of a fennel plant.

"Closer to the kitchen," she replied without hesitation. "That way it will be handy whenever anyone needs it."

They moved through the collection, each plant sparking a vision within Alice's mind's eye of how the château's grounds would transform. They discussed the best placement for the marjoram, the savory, the sage, and the parsley and organized the hibiscus, calendula, nasturtium, and dianthus while kneeling in the garden.

"This will be beautiful and practical, Alice," Marco said, brushing dirt off his hands as he stood up.

"I hope so. I keep thinking about the château's long history. I want the garden to tell a story as you move through it, starting with the roses and moving along to the basil and the chives. All of it will be edible."
Assuming I find all the hidden hemlock and get rid of it.

"Sounds perfect," Marco agreed. He extended his hand to help Alice up.

"You two better clean up." Sophie walked out into the garden accompanied by Jean-Baptiste. "It's nearly time to leave for the wine fest."

"Right!" Alice said. She could imagine what she looked like in her gardening clogs and overalls. "Give me ten minutes."

It was closer to fifteen by the time she returned to the garden wearing a pair of slim-fitting dark trousers with a white t-shirt under a linen jacket. She had a scarf draped around her neck that could add extra warmth if the day turned chilly. Marco had on jeans and an untucked button-down shirt, his dark hair curling onto his collar. She stopped for a second in the doorway as her heart did a little flipflop. She was going to a wine fest in Provence with a handsome man who cared about the same things she cared about. How lucky could one woman get?

Jean-Baptiste ushered them all into the car and they were off with a party atmosphere in the car.

"Sophie, is there a reason Château DuPont isn't participating in the wine fest?" Alice asked.

Sophie pursed her lips and then shrugged. "I don't want to speak ill of the dead, but René wasn't exactly the most popular vintner in the area. He had a way of rubbing people the wrong way."

Jean-Baptiste snorted as if that was an understatement.

"At any rate," Sophie continued. "He might not have been invited or might have decided not to participate himself. He didn't always include me in those kinds of decisions."

"At a loss for Château DuPont," Jean-Baptiste said. "Sophie has better sense in both business and wine-making than René ever did, in my opinion."

A slight flush crept up Sophie's cheeks. "Thank you, Jean-Baptiste. I didn't know you'd noticed that."

"Everyone notices that," he said, giving her a quick glance and then returning his gaze to the road.

Interesting. Maybe that was the source of the glances between Jean-Baptiste and Lilou. It would make sense. They were privy to a lot of the workings of the château and would know whether or not René had been a good steward of his family's business and legacy.

When they arrived, the town square buzzed with activity. Vendors flaunted wine-related wares while a live band crooned jazz tunes that danced on the breeze. Stands adorned with bottles of every hue ranged from deep burgundy to pale gold, inviting connoisseurs to sample the fruits of local labor.

"Look at this place," Sophie said, her eyes sweeping over the festivities.

"Isn't it wonderful?" Alice responded, feeling the music sway through her. She caught Marco's eye, and he grinned.

"Yes," he said. "Magical, in fact. Let's see what's here and enjoy the music," Marco suggested, taking her hand.

Sophie and Jean-Baptiste both excused themselves. Sophie to hobnob with another vintner she spotted across the square and Jean-Baptiste to meet a handsome young man who waved to him from near the bandstand.

Alice and Marco strolled toward the heart of the festivities, where a grand tent billowed like the sails of a majestic ship anchoring the town square. The structure, swathed in rich burgundy and cream fabric, buzzed with the excited chatter of wine enthusiasts eager to savor the expertise within. It was the guided wine-tasting adventure led by Geoffrey Lambert.

"Shall we?" Alice gestured towards the entrance. "Maybe I'll get some ideas of what else to plant that will go with Château DuPont's rosé.

"Sounds delightful," Marco replied, his broad-shouldered silhouette cutting through the crowd.

Inside, Geoffrey Lambert presided over an audience captivated by his every word. With a flourish of his hand, he unveiled bottles with labels as elegant as his tailored suit. "Now, this vintage," he began, his voice carrying above the murmur of the crowd, "pairs beautifully with a pissaladière or a delicate seafood dish."

Alice leaned in closer, absorbed Lambert's recommendations. "What would you think of a salad with dianthus blossoms in it to add a little spice to that menu?" she asked Marco in a low voice.

"Definitely a possibility. Nasturtiums are a possibility, too," Marco whispered back, his warm breath tickling her ear. "I'm still thinking about rose petal jam to go with a cheese course, though."

"Right." Alice went up on her tippy toes to try to get a better look.

"Let's get a little closer, shall we?" Marco suggested

Together, they edged nearer to Lambert, whose passion for wine was almost palpable as he described the balance of tannins and the whisper of oak that rounded each sip and how different foods could enhance certain flavors and clash with others.

"Remember," Lambert concluded with a charismatic smile, "wine is more than a beverage; it's a conversation between earth and artisan, a story told in flavors and aromas."

Alice sucked in a breath. It was the same way she felt about gardens.

"Quite the showman, isn't he?" Marco mused, a note of respect threading his voice.

"Indeed," Alice agreed, her gaze lingering on Lambert. Clearly, wine was this man's passion. His excitement over showing people what foods went with what wines had put two spots of color high on his cheeks. If someone ridiculed him or made others doubt his taste, would it be enough for him to commit murder?

Marco edged them even closer to the table. "Monsieur Lambert, my companion and I were thinking about a salad with dianthus flowers in it to go with the seafood entree you suggested and perhaps a rose petal jam to go with the cheese. Would that enhance these pairings? Or would the flavors clash?"

Lambert looked down at Marco, a surprised smile on his face. "I think those are excellent suggestions. I hadn't thought of flowers as part of the pairings. What an exciting approach."

Marco shrugged, his broad shoulders straining at his dress shirt. "Edible flowers are kind of my thing." He stuck out his hand. "Marco Bellamy."

"Geoffrey Lambert." Lambert shook Marco's hand. "What brings you to Provence, Monsieur Bellamy."

"I was hired by René DuPont to develop food pairings for the upcoming rosé competition," Marco said.

A murmur rippled through the crowd as Lambert's face darkened, the jovial facade slipping like wine from a tilted glass. "DuPont?" The word came out as a growl, the name seeming to sour on his tongue. "That man was a fraud—nothing but a pretentious poseur! Provence and its vineyards are better off now that he's gone."

Alice felt a chill despite the warm buzz of the festival around them. Her eyes narrowed, watching as the sommelier's hands clenched into fists at his sides, his polished exterior cracking under the pressure of old grievances.

"That seems quite harsh, Monsieur Lambert," Alice said.

"Harsh? Harsh is when someone who knows nothing about wine uses his family name to smear another's." Lambert glared down at her.

"Mr. Lambert," Alice interjected, her voice calm yet probing, "where were you on the night René DuPont was murdered?"

The question hung heavy in the tent, the jazz music outside clashing with the sudden tension. With an abrupt sweep of his arm, Lambert pointed towards the exit. "Out!" he barked. "I will not be interrogated at my own event!"

As they were ushered out of the tent by two burly men in black Polo shirts, Marco and Alice found themselves face to face with Inspector Fournier, who stood with arms crossed, observing the festivities with cool detachment.

"Mademoiselle Bloom. Monsieur Bellamy." Fournier nodded. "May I ask what you're doing here?"

"Enjoying the wine fest," Marco said, gesturing around them.

"And causing quite the stir, I see." Fournier glanced around them at the wine pairing tent.

"Inspector," Alice ventured, "are you here looking into Lambert's connection to the murder? He hated René. Marco mentioned DuPont's name in passing and Lambert became enraged."

Fournier's gaze was steely, his lips pressed into a thin line. "Miss Bloom, I do not discuss ongoing investigations with civilians."

"Then maybe you can tell us whether you've discovered the poison used to kill DuPont?" she persisted. "Was it something botanical? Could it have come from the garden at Château DuPont?"

"Miss Bloom," Fournier said, his tone a warning, firm like well-trodden earth, "the details of the case are confidential. And I'd advise you to refrain from digging where you might not like what you find. I understand you want to shift the blame for Monsieur DuPont's death to someone besides you and Monsieur Bellamy. That doesn't give you the right to accuse others."

He gave her a curt nod and strode off.

Alice stared after him. Shift the blame? That meant he still suspected her and Marco still. As she and Marco walked away, the vibrant notes of jazz that had her swaying to the music earlier felt dissonant and menacing.

As they navigated through the throng of festivalgoers, Marco's stride matched Alice's in rhythm but not in mood. He glanced at her, his brown eyes searching hers for an answer he wasn't sure he wanted to hear. "Alice," he began, the jovial cadence of earlier gone from his voice, "was checking out Lambert the real reason you wanted to come to the wine fest?"

She hesitated, taking a breath that filled her lungs with the soft afternoon air mingling with the scent of fermenting grapes. "Yes," she admitted, her gaze steady on the cobblestone path before them.

"Then why didn't you tell me?" The question hung between them like a delicate vine, ready to snap under too much tension.

"Because you waved off my concerns about Claire LeBlanc," Alice replied, hating to bring up disagreements when they'd been enjoying each other so much. "I didn't think you'd take this seriously either."

Marco dropped his head. "I'm sorry if you think I wasn't taking you seriously. How did you even know about Lambert's grudge against DuPont?"

Alice bit her lip. She knew Marco wasn't going to like what she was about to say, but she wasn't going to lie about it. "Scott told me. He invited me for coffee yesterday to tell me that he'd heard rumors about a grudge between Lambert and René."

Marco's expression tightened, like the twist of a vine around a trellis. "You met with Scott? I thought you were buying plants?" He struggled to keep his voice level.

"I was. I had coffee with Scott afterwards." Alice kept her voice absolutely level, too.

"Without telling me?" He put his hands on his hips and straightened those broad shoulders of his.

"Telling you? Marco, I don't need to report my movements to you," Alice said. "You have no claim over me."

Before he could respond, Sophie and Jean-Baptiste appeared, their approach cutting short any chance for further discussion. "Ready to head back?" Sophie asked, her smile wilting slightly as she sensed the change in atmosphere.

"Absolutely," Alice replied, forcing cheerfulness into her tone .

The ride back to Château DuPont was a silent affair, the party atmosphere gone. The car's interior felt cramped, heavy with unspoken words and the sour tang of tension. The landscape rolled by, rows of vines standing sentinel in the afternoon light as the day's festivities faded into the rearview mirror.

CHAPTER FOURTEEN

Once they returned to the château, everyone went their separate ways. Sophie to the winery, Jean-Baptiste to the garage, Marco to the kitchen, and Alice back to the garden.

She got to work planting the herb garden. When she was done, she stood back and couldn't stop herself from smiling. It was beautiful, if she did say so herself. Plus it smelled delicious. Thyme and sage. Marjoram and fennel. Basil and rosemary. She could only imagine the amazing dishes Marco would be able to make with it.

Marco, who might not be speaking to her at the moment. Alice felt a pang. Maybe she should have warned Marco about why she wanted to go to the wine fest and who had told her about it. Yet the idea of him wanting her to tell him where she was going and who she was meeting galled her. Scott had never much cared what she was doing. She was realizing that that cut both ways. Marco cared. But that also meant that he cared.

It was nearly time to change for dinner. She headed upstairs, her heart heavy. She still had a little time, so she opened her computer and started a video chat with Jazz.

"How's it going?" Jazz asked, her smiling face filling the screen.

"Honestly? I'm not sure." Alice drummed her fingers on the desk.

Jazz's smile faded. "Okay. Fill me in."

Alice did, telling her about Scott and Lambert and the tension between her and Marco. "It's like he expected me to ask his permission to meet Scott for coffee."

"Okay," Jazz said, stretching out the word. "That's uncool. But maybe put yourself in his shoes for a moment. How would you feel if he was off meeting his former lover in secret?"

Alice threw her hands in the air. "It wasn't a secret. I just didn't tell him."

"Listen to yourself, just for a minute." Jazz regarded her solemnly from the computer screen.

Alice took a deep breath and blew it out. "I see it. You're right. I'll talk to him."

"Good!" Jazz clapped her hands. "Now let's talk about this Lambert guy. Did you check him out before you went?"

"I peeked at his social media stuff. There were lots of photos of him at different wine tasting events."

"Anything for the night DuPont was murdered?" Jazz asked.

"Not that I could see."

"Let's see what else we can find." Jazz hit some buttons and shared her screen. She put Lambert's name into a search bar, reams of results poured in. "Whoa. This is an embarrassment of riches."

The first few entries were basic bio information. Nothing that either damned him or made him more of a suspect.

"Here's an article he wrote about local wineries," Jazz said. She pulled it up on her screen, and both she and Alice scanned through it.

"There!" Alice said. "He talks about Château DuPont.

"I've tasted paint thinner that had more flavor and complexity than these overly oaked, one-dimensional monstrosities. Every single wine they make is utterly forgettable, with nothing but harsh, unbalanced flavors that left a nasty aftertaste. "

"Ouch!" Jazz said. "Looks like he was getting his revenge in other ways than murder."

"It still doesn't rule him out, Jazz. You should have seen the look on his face when we mentioned DuPont's name. There was some real hatred there," Alice said.

"Let's see what else we can find." Jazz went back to the search results and began clicking through. There was another article where Lambert's name was mentioned. Jazz hit the link for it and a brightly lit photo of Lambert, standing before an attentive crowd, a glass of red wine held aloft came up. "He was doing a wine tasting presentation that evening."

Alice leaned closer, looking at the details about the event. Lambert would have been hard-pressed to get to the château and administer poison to René that evening. Her heart sank a little. She felt as though they were pruning away suspects without getting any closer to the root of the mystery.

"Looks like he had quite the audience," Alice remarked, trying to mask her disappointment. "No sneaking away unnoticed from that."

Jazz turned off the screen sharing and nodded. "Seems Lambert has an alibi as robust as a full-bodied Bordeaux." She shut down the avenue of suspicion with a click of her mouse.

"So now what?" Alice asked.

"Did you check out your other suspect? What did you say her name was?" Jazz asked.

"Claire LeBlanc." Alice leaned forward as Jazz went back to screen sharing and began searching.

There were several articles about the château and its wines and the occasional quote from Claire in various wine magazines. "This isn't getting us anywhere," Alice said.

"Hold your horses," Jazz said. "Let's take a look at her social media."

She scrolled through, looking at photos. It was still much more of the same, all wine-related.

"Wait! Hold on. Here's a notification about a photo on someone else's page, something she was tagged in."

Alice squinted at the screen. "Jazz that's from four years ago."

Jazz clicked on it. Alice's screen filled with a photo of Marco Bellamy with his arm around Claire LeBlanc, looking very chummy indeed. What. The. Actual. Heck. Marco knew Claire? Well enough to stand there with his arm around dher?

"Well, that explains a lot," Alice said. "Marco has been trying to steer me away from looking at LeBlanc from the beginning." It also explained why he wouldn't go with her to the wine tasting there. Claire would undoubtedly have recognized him.

"Maybe there's an innocent explanation for it," Jazz said, wincing a little.

"Maybe there is," Alice said, her voice sounding dull. "I'm not sure it matters. This investigation is going nowhere. I have no idea where to look next and no clue who I should trust."

Jazz looked up toward the ceiling and squinted her eyes, a clear sign she was thinking hard. "Have you noticed anything unusual at the winery lately?"

"Nothing out of the ordinary," Alice admitted, but then paused. Maybe she wouldn't notice anything because she didn't fully understand the nuances of the estate's daily operations. "But maybe I need to look closer, see things from a different angle. Learning about winemaking could provide some new clues or possibilities. Perhaps Sophie can shed some light on recent events."

"Looking for something recent would be good. I understand why you suspected both Lambert and LeBlanc, but both of them have had those grudges for a while. Why act on them now?" Jazz asked. "Plus, it sounds like Claire and René had buried the proverbial hatchet."

"You're right," she conceded, the realization dawning on her that time had perhaps diluted the bitterness of past conflicts. "Now, however, I think I need to go talk to Marco."

"Good luck, Alice." Jazz waved and ended the call.

She'd need it, but she was determined to clear the air between her and Marco. She put on fresh clothes and made her way to the kitchen where Marco and Lilou were working together to prepare dinner.

"Marco, could I speak to you for a moment?" Alice asked.

"Certainly," he said, not turning from the stove.

"I'd like to talk to you about Claire LeBlanc." She kept her voice even though she felt anything but.

Marco jerked and sloshed broth onto the stovetop. "I'm sure Claire LeBlanc has nothing to do with this mess."

Lilou, who had been quietly prepping a tray of hors d'oeuvres, set them down and wiped her hands on her apron. "I'll leave you two to discuss your theories. The table won't set itself." With a smile that didn't quite reach her eyes, she exited the room, the soft click of the door punctuating her departure.

Alice noted Marco's furrowed brow and the way his gaze darted toward the doorway through which Lilou had vanished. Marco set the wooden spoon down with a clatter that seemed to echo around the suddenly too-quiet kitchen. He leaned back against the counter. His hands, normally so sure and steady as they crafted the most delicate of pastries or garnishes, were now fidgeting with the hem of his apron. "What is it you want to know?"

What was it she wanted to know? The truth would be a good starter. "How well do you know her, Marco? Jazz and I were doing some research on her and we . . . We found a photo of the two of you together."

"I should have mentioned this earlier," he said, his voice a low rumble that seemed out of place in the cheerfully lit room. "When I first came to Château DuPont, years ago, Claire LeBlanc and I... we got to know each other quite well."

Alice took a second to process his words. "Got to know how well?" She tilted her head.

"More than friends," Marco admitted, his gaze dropping to the floor before locking onto hers once again. "After I left DuPont, I stayed with her for a while. It was a different time, a different life."

Alice's fair skin flushed with a mixture of surprise and something else—was it concern? "Why wouldn't you tell me this sooner, Marco?" Her voice was steadier than she felt, a testament to her years of negotiating delicate business deals in the competitive world of landscape design.

Marco ran a hand through his slightly too-long dark hair, a gesture

Alice had come to recognize as his way of collecting his thoughts. "It was so long ago, and it didn't seem relevant until all this... madness with René's murder started and then it felt like it was too late to say anything." He straightened up, the conviction in his voice firm. "But I need you to understand, Claire is passionate about her vineyard, about wine, but she's not a killer. I'm certain of it. You shouldn't waste your time suspecting her."

Alice absorbed his words, her mind racing like the vines at harvest, intertwining with new information and possibilities. She glanced at the bourguignon, the rich aroma reminding her that even the most complex flavors needed time to develop, just as this puzzle would require patience to solve.

Alice's fingers trailed along the counter's edge, her movements mechanical as she processed Marco's confession. The kitchen now seemed too close, the warmth from the oven mingling with a sudden chill that had settled in her heart. She reached for a dishtowel, dabbing at invisible spills on the countertop to keep her hands busy.

"I thought it was old news, and I didn't want to bother you with it," Marco said gently, hoping to soothe the sting.

"Bother me?" she echoed, the words leaving her mouth before she could catch them. Her hair fell across her face like a curtain, shielding her from the earnest concern in Marco's brown eyes. But it wasn't a shield against the embarrassment that crept up her neck and colored her cheeks.

She felt foolish. Now she knew the reason behind some of the shared glances between Lilou and Jean-Baptiste and knowing looks she'd seen. How many times had she walked through the château, greeted by smiles she mistook for friendliness, but were actually people laughing at her? Had her passion for plants made her oblivious to the human garden around her, where secrets bloomed in whispers and nods?

"Let's not let this spoil our evening," Marco suggested, reaching out to tuck a stray lock behind her ear.

But the gesture only heightened Alice's sense of isolation. She wanted so much to lean into it, to accept the comfort and warmth offered. Instead, she stepped back, withdrawing into herself. "I think I'll take my dinner in my room tonight," she said, her voice hollow but polite. "Long day. Need some time to think."

Marco's hand hovered in the air, uncertainty flickering across his face. "Alice, please—"

"Thank you for understanding." She cut him off before he could offer any more assurances or apologies. With the same precision she used to prune an overgrown rosebush, she excised herself from the situation, leaving behind the comfort of shared cooking and the promise of a shared meal.

Despite the enticing scents of thyme and garlic that filled the kitchen, the idea of sitting across from Marco, pretending that everything was fine while everyone watched her reaction, was more than she could bear. She needed space, time to untangle the knotted feelings within her.

She scooped up a bowl of the bourguignon and went upstairs.

In her room, the soft rustle of leaves against the window served as a reminder of the sanctuary she found in nature. Unlike people, plants never held hidden pasts or unexpected revelations. They were constant, reliable companions.

Sitting alone with a plate of bourguignon, she chewed slowly, tasting little. The food was delicious, no doubt, a testament to Marco's skill, but the flavors turned bland against the backdrop of her ruminations. Tonight, she dined not for pleasure, but for sustenance, seeking strength for what lay ahead. And as night deepened, like the roots of an ancient oak, so did her resolve to uncover the truth, no matter how personal the cost.

CHAPTER FIFTEEN

The next morning, Alice stepped into the winery with the morning sun. The air was rich with the scent of fermenting grapes.

"Good morning, Alice," Sophie greeted her with a bright smile. "What can I do for you?"

"I was hoping you could teach me a little bit more about rosé and how it's made."

"Absolutely. Let's start over here." Alice followed Sophie through rows of steel tanks, their surfaces cool and smooth under her fingers.

Sophie gestured toward a vat marked with today's date. "We're actually gearing up to bottle this batch for the upcoming rosé competition." Her eyes shone with a mixture of anticipation and pride.

"Is it ready then?" Alice asked, peering into the vat expecting finality.

"Nearly," Sophie said, tapping her chin thoughtfully. "There's always room for a few last-minute tweaks. You see, unlike its red counterparts, rosé isn't meant to age. It's a wine best enjoyed in the blush of youth."

"Ah, I see," Alice nodded, absorbing the nuance of Sophie's words. She couldn't help but draw parallels to her own work—gardens were much like wine, with some plants crafted to be savored in the moment and others evolving with time.

"It all starts with the grapes, of course," Sophie said. "We're using a blend of Grenache, Mourvèdre, and Cinsault. We harvest a bit earlier than we do for our red wines, when the skins have developed color but the fruit is still relatively low in sugar."

"So it won't get too sweet?" Alice asked.

"Exactly." Sophie nodded. "Then the grapes are crushed, but we try to keep the skin contact to a minimum. We try to control for color as well as flavor. The wine is fermented without the skins in these stainless steel tanks."

"And after that?" Alice asked.

"Then it's clarifying, stabilizing, and bottling. That's where we are now." Sophie patted a steel vat with fondness.

Alice couldn't see anything in what Sophie had said that would provide a clue to what had happened to René. It was all interesting, though.

"Let's taste, shall we? I can show you how we decide what blends to use and why," Sophie offered, reaching for two glasses and a thief, a long pipette used to draw wine from the barrel. She put a little of the pale pink liquid into a glass and handed one to Alice. "Tell me what you taste."

The wine was crisp, its flavor notes an intricate dance on Alice's palate. She took another sip, holding it in her mouth for a moment. Eyes closed, she let the flavors open and blossom on her tongue. "Maybe some strawberry and raspberry? But there's something floral, too, and maybe something a little bit citrusy?"

"Very good," Sophie said. "That's a great description of a classic Provence rosé. Do you like it?"

"It's lovely," Alice said sincerely, recognizing the dedication it took to reach such delicate balance.

"Thank you," Sophie responded, her expression softening. "Each bottle is like sending out a piece of myself into the world."

Both women stood there for a moment, so different in their crafts, yet united by the desire to leave a lasting impression through their creations. Today, in the sanctuary of grapevines and budding rosé, they found common ground, a shared passion blooming silently between them.

Sophie leaned against a table, her gaze fixed on the rows of bottles that gleamed under the soft light of the winery. "I've poured everything into this vintage," she confided, her fingers lightly tracing the curve of the glass in her hand. "This rosé has to be more than just good; it needs to be exquisite."

Alice watched as Sophie's eyes sparkled with a blend of determination and hope. In the cool air of the cellar, she could sense the weight of expectation hanging between the stacked barrels.

"Winning the competition could change my life," Sophie continued, her voice steady but with an undercurrent of urgency. "If I can clinch it with this batch, René's daughter might keep me on to manage the vineyard full-time. And even if she doesn't, a victory would make finding a new job much easier."

Alice sipped her wine again, appreciating the stakes for Sophie. A win here wasn't just about prestige; it was about security, about the future.

"And you know," Sophie added, setting down her glass with a resolve that resonated in the cool, quiet winery, "the winner sets the trends. It's not just about the medal or the accolades. It's about influence. When the experts declare a wine excellent, every vintner looks to mimic its style. It's like... creating a legacy that will guide the path of winemakers for years to come."

"Creating a legacy," Alice repeated softly, the idea resonating with her own dreams for the gardens she designed. She imagined the rosé, a delicate hue in a glass, leading the way just as her gardens might one day set a new standard for sustainable beauty.

"Exactly," Sophie said, a steely glint in her eye as she picked up a clipboard and made a note. "And legacies? They last. They're what we leave behind, the mark we make on the world. This wine will be my mark."

Alice nodded, feeling the depth of Sophie's passion mirror her own ambitions. As they stood in the heart of the winery, surrounded by the fruits of Sophie's labor, the scent of oak and grape hinting at the promise of the future, she realized how much they both longed to plant seeds of change that would bloom long after their time.

Alice strolled through the rows of aging vats, her fingers brushing against the cool steel as she pondered Sophie's words about legacy. The concept wasn't foreign to her; gardens were her canvas, and every design she etched into the earth was a testament to her vision—a vision that would flourish and evolve with each passing season.

"Legacy is what drives us," Alice said, her voice echoing slightly in the vast space. "Like your wine, my garden designs are more than just today's work. They're meant to thrive, to offer beauty and sanctuary years down the line."

Sophie nodded in agreement, pausing. "That's why you must continue with René's plans for the garden. It was his dream to see it completed, and I believe his daughter will want to honor that. His ideas about the garden and how it would work with the wine were among the best he ever had."

They wandered past the fermentation tanks, the gentle hum of machinery blending with the subtle scent of fermenting grapes. Sunlight filtered through high windows, casting dappled light on the concrete floor. Dust motes danced in the beams, and the air felt heavy with expectation.

"Speaking of the garden," Alice began, her eyes catching sight of a cluster of tables and chairs tucked away in a shadowy corner of the winery. "Those pieces there, could they be used in the garden? I think their mismatched charm would complement the casual atmosphere I'm aiming for."

Sophie followed her gaze and smiled. "Charming indeed. They've seen many harvest celebrations but have been retired for newer ones. Jean-Baptiste can move them out for you—give them a good rinse first, though. We wouldn't want any eight-legged surprises among the guests."

"Perfect," Alice replied, her mind already envisioning the eclectic seating nestled amongst the flowering shrubs and winding pathways. "It'll add such character to the space."

"Then it's settled. You keep designing your legacy, Alice, and I'll focus on perfecting mine in this bottle." She paused for a moment, then asked, "So tell me, what exactly happened at the wine fest? There was definitely some tension between you and Marco when we headed home."

"Ah, yes," Alice sighed, turning to face her. The memory of the afternoon was still fresh, tinged with the acrid taste of unease. "We went to see Geoffrey Lambert's presentation. He got seriously angry when he found out Marco and I were working for René."

Sophie's brow furrowed, a shadow of concern passing over her features. "He never hid his disdain for René. Lambert felt overshadowed, under appreciated. It's no secret they clashed on more than one occasion."

"I thought maybe Lambert could have hated René enough to poison him," Alice said.

Shock registered on Sophie's face, stark and unfiltered, before she composed herself once more. "That's a heavy accusation, Alice. But given Lambert's temper..."

"I know," Alice interjected, feeling the weight of her own suggestion. "It doesn't matter. He has an alibi. He was miles away in front of dozens of people."

Sophie walked back toward the laboratory. "Even if Geoffrey Lambert had been in town, René would never accept a drink from him, not after all those scathing reviews."

"They hated each other that much? Alice asked. She'd been focused on how Lambert felt about DuPont, not the other way around.

Sophie leaned back against the lab bench. "Absolutely," she said with a nod. "René had a nose for grudges as well as grapes."

Alice studied Sophie, noticing the determination etched into the lines of her face. She realized that beneath Sophie's calm exterior lay a reservoir of knowledge about the vineyard and its people—information that could be crucial. As much as Alice was adept at reading the needs of her plants, perhaps Sophie, too, had her own ways of discerning the secrets hidden within the rows of vines and the hearts of those who tended them.

"So who should I turn my attention to now? Is there anyone else around here who had a particularly sour taste for René?"

"Actually, yes," Sophie replied, her voice taking on a softer timbre. "René could be . . . difficult. His family had been here a long time, and he felt entitled to a certain amount of respect and deference."

"So he made enemies?" Alice asked. "Beyond Lambert and DeBlanc?"

Sophie nodded. "Lucille Girard comes to mind. She's that botanist. She was working on developing a new hybrid grape. Thought it could be a game-changer for winemakers."

Alice tilted her head, intrigued. "And René didn't take kindly to this innovation?"

"Far from it," Sophie said, her eyes widening. "He accused her of trying to sabotage his vineyard. Claimed her hybrid grapes would cross-pollinate with his and ruin his crop."

"Quite the accusation," Alice noted, her mind already turning over the implications. The idea of Lucille Girard having a motive rooted itself firmly in her thoughts. René Dupont, with his proud legacy, might just have underestimated the potential wrath of a scientist scorned.

"It was." Sophie glanced toward the window, where the vineyards stretched out like green waves. "René had a way of making enemies with words as easily as he did friends with wine."

Alice sat down in the lab's swivel chair, her gaze fixed on Sophie. "But wouldn't cross-pollination be highly unlikely? Grapevines are predominantly self-pollinating plants. The chance of Lucille's hybrids affecting René's vineyard should be minimal."

Sophie nodded, a wry smile playing at the corners of her mouth. "Exactly. But René wasn't one to let facts get in the way of a good story, especially if it could discredit someone else's work." She paused. "You know, for all his bluster about lineage and terroir, René was more showman than scholar."

"Are you saying he was more about theatrics than actual viticulture knowledge?" Alice arched an eyebrow, intrigued by this new perspective on the man whose death had cast a shadow over the picturesque estate.

"Let's just say he knew enough to impress those who knew less," Sophie replied with a shrug. "But when it came to the science of winemaking, well, he'd often confuse tannins with tantrums."

Alice chuckled, appreciating the candid insight. It painted a picture of a man who had built his reputation on tradition rather than innovation—a stark contrast to the passionate dedication she saw in her own work with plants and Sophie's dedication to her rosé.

"His accusations must have hit Lucille hard then," she said, her voice tinged with empathy. "To be publicly humiliated over something so... improbable. It would take more than bees to upset the genetic makeup of a vineyard."

"Indeed, it did," Sophie confirmed, her face sobering as she considered the impact on Girard's career. "And in a small community like this, where word travels faster than pollen on a breeze, reputations are everything."

"Sounds like Lucille had motive, but what about opportunity and means?" Alice concluded, her mind already racing ahead to the next step in unraveling the mystery. Perhaps the key to solving René's murder lay not among the vines but within the hearts of those he had wronged. "Maybe I'll pay her a visit. See if I can learn more about this hybrid she's creating."

"Let me know if I can do anything else to help. I'd like to find out who murdered René, too. I really think we could win this rosé competition and I'd hate to have his death cast a shadow over that. But first," Sophie said. "Lunch."

CHAPTER SIXTEEN

Alice and Sophie walked out of the winery and toward the château. Alice was still deep in thought about what Sophie had told her. She wanted to talk to Lucille Girard, but in a way that didn't threaten her. Perhaps botanist to botanist. How to set that up, though?

She took two more steps when the answer hit her. "Sophie, you go ahead. I need to make a quick phone call. I'll be in in a moment."

"Of course." Sophie left Alice underneath one of the trees and Alice pulled out her cellphone and hit the button to make a call. "Professor Greenway? It's Alice Bloom again."

"How nice to get to talk to you so often! What can I do for you?"

Alice could hear the smile in her teacher's voice. "I need to get in touch with Lucille Girard, she's a botanist here in Provence. I want to see what she's doing with hybrids. I was hoping your connections in the plant world might help me secure an invitation."

"Lucille, eh? We haven't met personally, but I know people who know her." The professor's voice held a note of curiosity. "I might just have the right contacts for that. Let me see what I can do."

"Thank you, Professor. I owe you one."

"Consider it a debt paid in full if you can untangle this mystery you've found yourself in," Professor Greenway replied with a hint of excitement.

"Will do, Professor. And I'll keep you updated," Alice promised, her spirits lifted. With the phone call concluded, she continued into the château where the group had already assembled in the dining room.

The rustle of envelopes and the soft thud of a package hitting the oak dining table announced the arrival of the post. Lilou, with her usual grace, distributed the assortment among the residents of the château, pausing as she came upon an envelope with Alice's name scrawled across it.

"Here you are, Alice," Lilou said, handing her the letter with a slight furrow in her brow. "This one's got no return address."

Alice glanced up and took the letter, her fingers tracing the edges as if to decipher its origins before even breaking the seal. The paper felt coarse, the handwriting was rushed—angry, even.

"Odd," Alice muttered, sliding a finger under the flap and tearing it open. A single sheet fell out, landing on the table with an ominous silence that seemed to demand attention. She unfolded it and read the message, her lips parting ever so slightly as the words sunk in.

"Stop asking questions."

"Who would send something like this?" Lilou asked, leaning in to inspect the menacing note.

"Anonymous threats—the last resort of a desperate soul." Alice tried to keep her tone light, but her heart raced at the thought of being on the radar of someone who might have already killed someone. She examined the postmark closely. "It was mailed yesterday from town."

"Town? That narrows it down, doesn't it?" Lilou's eyes were sharp, observant. "Who knows about your little detective endeavor?"

"Other than everyone here?" Alice began ticking off on her fingers. "There's Claire LeBlanc and Geoffrey Lambert. But Lambert isn't the murderer. He has an alibi."

"LeBlanc, though?" Lilou interjected, dark brows raised.

"Hasn't truly been ruled out, but unlikely." Alice glanced sideways at Marco, who kept his face impassive. She tapped the letter against the table, her mind racing with possibilities. "But you're right. It's a small community. Word travels faster than a vine weevil on a grapevine."

"Especially when it's juicy gossip about a murder investigation." Lilou's voice carried a note of concern. "And what about your plant circles? They're close-knit, too."

"Very much the same. Passionate people connected by their love for botany." Alice sighed, folding the letter and tucking it into her pocket. "I suppose anyone could have caught wind of my snooping around."

"Be careful, Alice," Lilou warned, her hand briefly touching Alice's arm. "This letter is proof enough that you're stirring the pot—and not everybody appreciates the taste of truth."

"Truth is an acquired taste," Alice replied with a wry smile, feeling the weight of the threat but refusing to let it dampen her resolve. "But one I'm quite fond of."

Alice thanked Marco for the lovely lunch and told the group she was going to take a brief nap. She still wasn't accustomed to day drinking, but the Cabernet Franc Marco had served with the cheese course had been hard to decline.

She ascended the staircase of the château, her mind a garden of worry, the letter's threat taking root among her thoughts. She entered her room, a cozy haven lined with botanical prints and soft, sage-green walls that usually comforted her. Today, however, not even the familiar scent of lavender and rosemary could soothe her ruffled spirits.

She perched on the edge of her bed and opened her laptop. The screen flickered to life and Alice clicked the icon on her laptop screen, initiating the video call. Daisy's face appeared, her features framed by curtains of eco-friendly fabric that Alice knew were dyed with natural indigo. Just seeing her sister's face made her smile.

"Hey, sis," Alice greeted, forcing a smile.

"Ali, you look worried. What's going on?" Daisy's voice carried the familiar tinge of concern as she leaned into the camera, her own stylish studio backdrop framing her face.

She'd been planning on just catching up for a few minutes. Talking to her sister always made her feel better. Leave it to Daisy to diagnose her mood with a single glance. Alice took a deep breath, her fingers absently tracing the edge of the letter that lay beside her keyboard. "I got this letter today," she said, holding it up to the camera. "It's not exactly fan mail."

Daisy squinted at the scrawled handwriting visible on the screen. "That looks... sinister. Please tell me you're packing your bags and coming home."

"Can't do that, Daisy." The resolve in Alice's voice was as sturdy as an oak tree. "Someone's trying to scare me off, but I'm not about to let them win. And Marco... I can't leave him to deal with this mess alone."

"Marco, huh?" Daisy's expression softened slightly. "How are things with the herb whisperer?"

Alice's lips curled into a half-smile at the nickname, but then she sighed. "Complicated, as usual. We don't know each other as well as I thought we did. Plus, Scott is in Provence, too."

"Scott?" Daisy's tone sharpened with disapproval. She'd never been one of his fans. "What does he want now?"

"Claims he's here for some rare orchid," Alice said.

"Ha!" Daisy apparently believed that about as much as Alice did. "And Marco? How's he taking all this?"

"We had an argument," Alice admitted, looking down at her hands. "Actually, I'm not sure it was an argument. He wasn't completely honest with me about some time he spent here in Provence a few years ago."

Daisy sighed, shaking her head. "So what are you going to do about those two?"

"Truthfully, I don't know," Alice confessed. "Scott keeps saying he's changed. But I feel such a connection with Marco, except now I don't know if I can trust him . . ."

"Well, you know my vote," Daisy said. "What I really want is for you to be happy, Ali. Whatever you decide, I've got your back 100%." She paused. "Just don't pick Scott, okay?"

Alice laughed. "I'm not picking anybody right now. I'm going to find out what happened to René DuPont and finish redesigning his garden. I've been working with his assistant vintner, Sophie. She's very supportive of my ideas."

"That's wonderful!" Then her face got serious. "Stay safe, okay?" Daisy's eyes were serious, but her tone still held the warmth of sisterly love.

"Always do," Alice replied.

"Um, not exactly. I seem to remember you ending up in an emergency room in Italy," Daisy pointed out.

Alice waved it away. "That was an isolated incident."

"Let's try to keep it that way, okay?" Daisy blew her a kiss.

Alice closed the laptop with a click, her mind already weaving through the tangled vines of her next move. Alice allowed herself a twenty-minute cat nap and then headed back out into the garden. She'd pulled out the old plants and then amended the soil for the edible flowers. Now, it was just a matter of putting them in.

She glanced over her shoulder at the kitchen. She wanted Marco's input on placement and overall design, but things were so tense between them. The more she thought about it, the more her dander got up again. He was not the boss of her. Who was he to tell her who she could have coffee with? Especially when he wasn't being fully transparent.

Sighing, she sank down onto the ground. They hadn't really said what they were to each other or made any kind of commitments, but she knew how she felt about him and was pretty sure she knew how he felt about her. There just always seemed to be obstacles between them, not the least of which was geographical. Who knew where her next assignment would take her and for how long? He was in the same boat.

They were here now, though. Together. With a project that they could collaborate on. She was wasting time being upset with him.

Gathering her resolve, she stood and went to the kitchen door. She stepped in to find him already making preparations for dinner. It was one more way their work was similar. There was a lot of groundwork that had to be lain before the completed project could be presented and once one thing was finished, it was time for the next.

"Marco?" she said.

He turned from the counter. "Alice! Is everything all right?"

"Yes. Fine. More than fine, really. I have all those beautiful edible flowers to plant. The bed is ready. I was hoping you would have a minute to help me decide on how to arrange them." She looked over at the door frame, running her thumb down the edge of it.

"Of course!" He sounded delighted, and Alice's heart lightened a bit. "Now?"

"If you have time."

"Always for you, little blossom."

Hearing the nickname he'd given her back in Italy made her look over at him for real now. There he was, tall and strong and smiling at her. She smiled back. "Well, come on then." She beckoned him to follow her.

***

The sun had dipped below the horizon, casting a warm glow over everything. Alice and Marco had spent several hours deciding on how to arrange both the edible flower garden, working companionably side by side. He'd had to go back into the kitchen to finish making dinner, but she'd stayed out and planted as much as she could. There was still work to be done to prepare for the workers to come and pull out the yew hedges. Tomorrow would be a new day, a day closer to her goals.

She stripped off her gardening gloves and checked her phone for the gazillionth time. Still nothing from Professor Greenway.

As if she'd summoned her, the phone buzzed in her hand with the professor's name on the Caller ID. "Professor Greenway, any luck?"

"Indeed, Alice," came the warm, reassuring voice of her mentor. "Your appointment with Lucille Girard is set for tomorrow morning. I've told her you're seeking advice on plant genetics. She seemed rather eager to have a professional conversation."

A wave of relief washed over Alice, followed quickly by excitement. "That's brilliant, Professor. Thank you. I knew I could count on you."

"Remember, Alice," Greenway cautioned, "Lucille can be... particular. Go armed with your questions, but keep your eyes open. You never know what you might learn."

"Understood," Alice replied, her mind already racing through potential leads and angles of inquiry. "I'll let you know how it goes."

"Good luck, my dear. And be careful," said Greenway before ending the call.

Alice took a deep breath and gazed out over the garden. There was a lot of work to be done yet, but she felt good about having gotten started. The delicate fragrance of rosemary and thyme drifted through the air. Tomorrow she would step into Lucille Girard's world. She hoped there would be answers there, missing pieces of the puzzle of René DuPont's death.

She headed in to take a quick shower and get ready for whatever culinary delight Marco had prepared for them all tonight. Her investigation was blooming, and she couldn't wait to see what secrets tomorrow would unearth.

CHAPTER SEVENTEEN

Alice's gaze traced the undulating rows of vines, a patchwork quilt of green against the red clay soil, as Jean-Baptiste navigated the narrow road towards Lucille Girard's home. The car's windows were down, and the air was rich with the scent of ripening grapes and earth.

"How long have you worked for Château DuPont?" Alice asked. She hadn't missed the occasional long look between Jean-Baptiste and Lilou and suspected they knew more about what went on at the château than either of them let on.

"It's been around two years now," Jean-Baptiste said.

"Did you like working for René?"

"René, he was such a character," Jean-Baptiste began, his voice steady over the hum of the engine.

"How so?" Alice had only known René for a day or two before tragedy struck. She hadn't really gotten much of a sense of the man, and the things she'd been learning seemed at odds with the expansive, friendly man she'd met.

"He put a lot of energy into creating a certain personae." Jean-Baptiste glanced briefly over his shoulder at Alice, before focusing back on the road. "Maybe more than he put into anything else."

That description fit with what she was starting to learn about René. "So he wasn't quite the expert he wanted everyone to believe?"

"Certainly not on wine. Sophie is the one who really knows the dance of the grapes, the alchemy of fermentation. She has the knack, the education. She studied at the university in Bordeaux, you know."

"Really?" The Bordeaux Sciences Argo was the most respected viticulture and enology school in France. "René never mentioned that."

Jean-Baptiste chuckled. "He wouldn't. He enjoyed the spotlight too much. But Sophie, she's the one who turns those sun-kissed berries into bottled poetry. She's all about the wine."

"Did she mind René taking credit for her work?" Alice asked, frowning. She knew she wouldn't be too happy if Owen took credit for her designs.

Jean-Baptiste made a face, then said. "I don't think it was the credit she resented. He had a tendency to meddle. It frustrated her when she'd work hard to perfect something and he would come in at the last minute and make some adjustment she didn't approve of."

"That would be frustrating." It also called to mind what Marco had said about René meddling with spices at the last minute.

As they neared Girard's property, Alice felt a twinge of excitement mixed with apprehension. René's death had cast a shadow over everything she once admired about Provence.

"Here we are," Jean-Baptiste announced, pulling up to a stone wall crowned with cascading ivy.

Alice stepped out of the car, squinting as sunlight danced through the leaves. She took a deep breath, ready to untangle the roots of the mystery that lay hidden beneath the beauty of Provence. "I can't imagine I'll be too long. An hour at the most."

"I'll be right here," Jean-Baptiste said.

Alice thanked him and then stepped into the courtyard and knocked on the door to the main house.

The woman who answered the door was tall and elegant, her hair a mass of white curls framing a face etched with fine lines, a testament to her years of hard work in the outdoors. She wore an outfit not unlike Alice's own gardening clothes, but with a little touch of that French *je ne sais quoi* that Alice couldn't quite master.

"Alice Bloom?" she asked.

"Yes. Thank you for seeing me, Mademoiselle Girard."

"Please. Call me Lucille. Any student of Lily Greenway is welcome always in my home." Lucille's proffered hand was calloused and a bit rough, evidence of years spent tending to the land.

"I really appreciate you taking the time." Alice stepped through the arched doorway into Girard's home, a welcoming warmth enveloping her as the scent of lavender tickled her senses. The interior was as one with nature, flooded with light, and brimming with greenery that spilled from pots and planters in every corner.

"Professor Greenway speaks very highly of you," Lucille mentioned as they settled into a sunlit sitting area framed by windows that looked out onto a garden alive with the buzz of bees.

"Lily has been a guiding light," Alice replied, fondness for her mentor threading her words. "She's told me about your remarkable work with creating hybrids."

Lucille smiled. '"Lily's praise means the world, especially after... well, after everything."

"Speaking of plants," Alice ventured, wondering what Girard's reaction would be, "I've been pondering over hydrangeas. I'm wondering if it's possible to breed them to retain their color, regardless of soil acidity?"

Lucille tilted her head, considering the question. "Hydrangeas are a bit like people, aren't they? Influenced by their environment. You could try to breed them, but amending the soil would be simpler. And sometimes, it's best not to meddle too much with what nature intended."

Alice nodded. Nothing in Girard's demeanor suggested that she knew anything about the hydrangeas at Château DuPont. Of course, it was possible that the hydrangeas had nothing to do with René's death, that the sabotage of the plants was a completely separate issue.

Lucille Girard led the way, her steps sure and light as they descended a stone staircase into the lush embrace of her garden. Alice followed, her senses filling with the fragrant symphony of herbs and flowers that played upon the mild Provencal breeze. The path wound through beds of flowering thyme and rosemary, a natural tapestry that whispered secrets of sustainable cultivation.

"Oh!" Alice clasped her hands to her chest. "This is beautiful! The way you use your knowledge of the local flora is amazing. Do you mind if I take some notes? This is aspirational."

"Thank you," Lucille said, with a modest tilt of her head. "These plants are like old friends to me."

As they rounded a bend, Lucille's gaze found Alice's. "So tell me, what brings a landscape designer of your renown all the way to our little corner of Provence?"

Alice glanced at the vine-laden trellises that framed their walk. "I came here to assist René DuPont in preparing his gardens for the upcoming rosé competition. His assistant asked me to stay on to finish the work, despite what's happened."

The name hung between them like a dropped wineglass, its impact shattering the former ease. Lucille's expression clouded over, a storm brewing behind her eyes. Her pace slowed, and she turned to face Alice squarely, the full force of her agitation palpable.

"René DuPont," she uttered, the name laced with a bitterness that soured the air. "That man... he got exactly what was coming to him."

Alice felt a chill despite the warmth of the day. She studied Lucille's face, looking for the root of such sudden vehemence. The shadows of past grievances flickered there, dark vines entwined around Lucille's usually composed features.

"How so?" Alice asked, careful to keep her tone neutral, yet her mind raced with questions. What had transpired between Lucille and

René to elicit such a reaction?

"It just seems fitting that a man that put so much poison out in the world would die because of ingesting it himself." Lucille drew a deep breath, as if to calm herself, and gestured for Alice to continue walking.

Alice followed. "How do you mean that René put poison out into the world? Surely, you don't mean that literally."

"No. Not literally." Lucille shook her head. "He had a way of spreading accusations and rumors. While anyone who knew him well didn't respect his knowledge of winemaking or viticulture, his family has been around for a long time and his words held weight. Too much weight, if you ask me. Let's not waste any more time on that man, " she said, her voice clipped, yet controlled. "There's more I'd like to show you."

Alice nodded, following Lucille's lead once again, but now with a new awareness that beneath the serene beauty of these gardens lay stories untold and perhaps some thorns hidden among the blooms.

The revelation wove through Alice's thoughts, intertwining with her knowledge of plants, their uses, and misuses. Her eyes darted to Lucille's hands, soil-stained and honest, yet surely capable of concocting more than just criticism.

"Interesting," Alice murmured, filing away Lucille's words like seeds for later sowing.

They meandered along a pebble-lined path, the crunch beneath their feet mingling with the distant song of cicadas. The path forked, and Alice caught a glimpse of glass structures tucked away amidst a copse of trees—a greenhouse that seemed almost shy in its concealment.

"What's in there?" Alice asked, nodding towards the veiled sanctuary.

Lucille's stride didn't falter, but her gaze hardened. "Oh, just some propagation experiments. Nothing worth seeing, really." She steered Alice firmly toward the main path, her grip gentle but insistent on Alice's elbow.

"Propagation can be quite revealing," Alice pressed, her curiosity piqued like thorns on a rose stem.

"Perhaps another time," Lucille said, her smile not fully reaching her eyes. "Today, let's focus on the beauty that's already in full bloom."

As they continued onward, Alice couldn't help but wonder what secrets lay within that greenhouse, secrets as obscured as the motives behind René DuPont's untimely demise. Around her, though, the garden was a symphony of colors and aromas. Much of it looked natural and wild, but Alice could see the organizing principle beneath it all. It was exactly what she was hoping to achieve at Château DuPont.

"Lucille," Alice ventured, "I've been curious about hemlock. Is it prevalent here in Provence?"

"Ah, yes, hemlock," Lucille replied, bending to inspect a cluster of purplish flowers at their feet. "It grows all too well in these parts. Its invasive nature is quite the nuisance and dangerous, too. It's often mistaken for harmless plants like wild carrot. There have been several unfortunate incidents of accidental poisonings. Why do you ask?"

The weight of her words settled between them, and Alice thought of René, his life snuffed out so unexpectedly. Could it have been an innocent mistake? A tragic case of misidentification? Not murder at all?

"I found some in the gardens at Château DuPont," Alice said. "I wasn't sure if it was an isolated intruder or something I should be watching out for."

"Definitely watch out for it. So much of the plant is poisonous. It would be quite easy for someone to become quite ill or even die because of it," Lucille said.

Alice bit her lip. Lucille would definitely know hemlock and probably have a good idea of how to prepare it to give to someone else without harming herself. "Do you think René could have accidentally eaten some of it or been fed some of it? By someone with a grudge?"

Lucille's lips hardened into a thin line. "Are you suggesting something, Miss Bloom?"

"No," Alice said, refused to be cowed. "Just asking questions."

"Well, I think I'm done answering them. Allow me to escort you to the door." Lucille strode away, not even glancing to see if Alice was following.

With a final glance around the vibrant garden that felt more like a verdant labyrinth with hidden truths lurking beneath its beauty, Alice knew it was time to leave. As she walked back to Jean-Baptiste's waiting car, the warm Provençal breeze seemed to carry whispers of the secrets she had yet to uncover.

Could René's death have been just a tragic accident after all? The question hung in the air like the scent of grapes ripening on the vine, intoxicating and heady with possibilities.

CHAPTER EIGHTEEN

Alice stepped through the carved wooden door of Château DuPont, her mind still replaying the exchange with Lucille Girard. The rich aroma of simmering herbs and roasted vegetables greeted her, a comforting embrace after the morning's unsettling revelations. Marco and Lilou were a study in fluid motion around the kitchen, their hands dancing from pot to chopping board to oven with an easy rhythm.

"Can I help with anything?" Alice asked, going to the sink to wash her hands.

Lilou, with her usual grace under culinary pressure, pointed towards a basket of bell peppers and zucchini. "Could you chop these for the ratatouille?"

Alice nodded and reached for the knife, hoping the familiar act of slicing and dicing would ground her racing thoughts. She was aligning the vegetables on the cutting board when the front door chime echoed through the château. Lilou excused herself to answer the door and returned followed by the measured footsteps of Inspector Fournier entering the domain of simmering sauces and secret spices.

"Mademoiselle Bloom," he began, his gaze as penetrating as the questions she knew were coming. "I've just had a very interesting conversation with Mademoiselle Girard about hemlock."

"Ah," Alice said, pausing mid-chop. She placed the knife down and wiped her hands on the apron she'd tied around her waist. "Yes, I found some in the garden here."

"Is it easily recognizable?" Fournier inquired, his eyes scanning the room, resting for a moment on the array of herbs Marco had arranged on the counter.

"Many people confuse it with other harmless plants," Alice explained, her voice steady despite the flutter in her chest. "Queen Anne's lace or parsley or wild carrot, particularly to the untrained eye."

"Interesting," Fournier murmured, stroking his chin thoughtfully. "Yet you, Mademoiselle Bloom, did not mistake it for something benign. You recognized the hemlock in the DuPont garden immediately."

"Of course," Alice replied, meeting his gaze with confidence. "I'm a botanist. It's second nature for me to differentiate between plants, especially when one is as perilous as hemlock."

Fournier nodded, his hands clasped behind his back as he paced around the kitchen island. He paused, his eyes locking onto Marco, who was carefully inspecting a sprig of thyme. "And Monsieur Bellamy, with your expertise in herbs and cooking, would also be well aware of its dangers," he said, almost casually.

Marco looked up, his brown eyes clouded with concern. "Yes, I would probably recognize it," he admitted, his voice a quiet rumble. "But I never would've served such a thing from our garden."

"So you say." Fournier's tone was noncommittal as he gave them both another long, searching look. Then, without another word, he made his leave, the echo of his footsteps gradually fading into the distance.

The knife lay forgotten on the cutting board as Alice exchanged a troubled glance with Marco. The air seemed to grow heavy with unsaid thoughts and worries. Despite the flavorsome aroma of garlic and basil wafting through the air, there was now a subtle undercurrent of unease.

Alice picked the knife back up and slid it through a zucchini, the rhythmic chopping a counterpoint to the simmering tension that remained in the wake of Inspector Fournier's departure. The verdant scent of freshly cut greens mingled with the hearty notes of Marco's steak au poivre bubbling on the stove.

"Lucille Girard calling Fournier over my questions about hemlock so quickly," Alice said, her tone light but her hands gripping the knife handle a tad too tightly, "it makes me think she's trying to throw suspicion off herself and onto us."

Marco glanced over from where he was tenderly stirring the pot. "Which only makes her look more guilty, in my book."

"Mine, too." Alice frowned.

***

Later that night, after a full day's work in the garden, Alice perched at the edge of her desk chair, the soft glow of her laptop screen casting an eerie light across her room. In the stillness , the faint hum of the hard drive was a comforting companion to her late-night sleuthing.

With a few keystrokes, she navigated to a satellite imaging service and entered the address of Lucille Girard's property. The digital map zoomed in, revealing the sprawling estate from a bird's-eye view.

Alice's eyes darted across the screen until they settled on an open space—a structure ensconced behind a copse of trees, partially obscured from the casual observer. It was the greenhouse that Girard had so quickly steered her away from, its glass panes gleaming dully under the moonlight captured in the photograph.

"Gotcha," Alice murmured to herself, her lips curving into a half-smile . She wondered what secrets that cloistered glasshouse might hold. What was Lucille hiding among her cultivated greenery? She took a sip of cabernet franc.

Her mind buzzing with questions, Alice opened a new tab and began scouring the web for any recent publications or news about Girard's botanical endeavors. Bits and pieces of information formed a mosaic of Lucille's activities—conference attendances, forum discussions, even a mention in a local gardening club newsletter — that piece by piece coalesced into a picture that Alice could understand. One thing became clear: despite the public setback caused by René's accusations, Lucille was far from idle.

A particular article caught Alice's eye, one that spoke of ongoing research into plant hybrids. The terminology was dense, riddled with scientific jargon, but to Alice, it was familiar. She sat back and took a long look at her notes, thinking about which conferences Lucille had attended and what forum discussions she had participated in. Her heart rate picked up as she pieced together the implications. She leaned in closer, her hair falling like a curtain around her face, shielding her from everything but the revelation unfolding on her screen.

Alice' honed in on botanical journals and scholarly articles, all linked to Lucille Girard's name. A promising lead emerged from the digital tangle: Girard had pivoted sharply in her research. The hybrid grapes that once consumed her professional life were now old news. Instead, she was nurturing something new—something decidedly more profitable.

"Show me your secrets," Alice murmured, her gaze locked onto an abstract detailing the cultivation of a rare orchid variety, rumored to possess extraordinary medicinal properties. Alice had some experience with what the world of orchid collectors was like because of her time with Scott. Even when she'd been enmeshed with it, she'd been fairly certain that some of those collectors were, well, a bit crazy. The market for a bloom that was both rare and possessed healing capabilities would be astronomical, and Lucille, with her knack for plant genetics, stood at the forefront of this green gold rush.

She would certainly be able to thumb her nose at DuPont once she went wide with her research.

But as the pieces of the puzzle began clicking into place, Alice paused, her finger hovering above the trackpad. Girard as DuPont's murderer didn't make sense. If Girard harbored a vendetta against René DuPont for his scathing critique of her grape research, wouldn't she relish the chance to prove him wrong with her new venture? Moreover, if DuPont's dismissal of her past work propelled her towards this lucrative orchid breakthrough, it was he who inadvertently set her on the path to potential riches.

But what did all this mean about Girard's motive for murder? Surely, Girard's intellect would recognize that DuPont's criticism was a hidden blessing, a serendipitous push away from failure and towards fortune. A motive for murder it was not.

With a gentle click, Alice closed the tab on her computer, her resolve strengthening. Lucille Girard, despite her dislike for the late vintner, owed him a debt of gratitude, not the malice of a murderer. Alice needed to look elsewhere.

There was one other consideration as well. Maybe Scott hadn't been lying about his reasons for coming to Provence. She'd thought he was making up rumors about special orchids, but if she could put together what Girard was doing in an evening's worth of online research, others probably suspected it as well. If Scott was looking for special orchids, Provence should be top of his list. Did he know about Girard? He hadn't said her name. Sometimes rumors were like that, though. Hints here and there without specifics.

A soft tapping at the window interrupted Alice's thoughts. She stood and crossed her room, parting the curtains to peer outside. The garden was awash in silver light, every leaf and petal etched with moonlight. There, below her window, stood Scott, casting a long shadow on the dew-speckled grass.

"Scott?" she called out, a note of surprise in her voice. "What are you doing here?"

"Can we talk?" His voice drifted up to her, slightly plaintive.

Alice hesitated for a breath before unlatching the window and pushing it open wide. She leaned out, resting her elbows on the sill, the cool night air brushing against her face. Scott looked up at her, his blond hair almost glowing under the celestial glow. "What do you want to talk about?" she asked.

"Us," he said. The words seemed to hang between them, like the delicate tendrils of a vine reaching out.

Alice felt a flutter in her chest, an echo of what used to be the faint taste of his kiss. "Scott, there is no—"

"I know. There is no us right now. There could be, though. We could go back to the way it was." He cut her off, his voice tightening. "I've tried to forget, believe me, I have. But it's no use." He paused, taking a step closer to the house, his blue eyes locked on hers. "Leave this all behind. Come away with me."

"Scott, I—"

"Please," he interjected, the word soft but urgent. "There's another orchid lead, a rare one. I leave tomorrow."

She watched him, the earnestness in his gaze, the hope that she might just say yes. The nocturnal symphony of crickets played around them, and for a moment, the world seemed suspended in time.

Alice squared her shoulders. "Scott, unlike you, I don't just up and leave people behind," she said, her voice firm like the steady trunk of an old oak tree.

He shifted uneasily, his lanky form a stark contrast to the orderly rows of hedges behind him. "Alice, I—"

"Listen," she interrupted, her tone softened by the years of growth since she'd woken up to only a note on a dresser in Morocco. "I've worked hard for the life I have now. My garden designs, my clients— they're all part of who I am."

The moonlight highlighted the dew-kissed petals of the roses below. Her passion for the natural world was not something she could abandon, not even for the wild allure of chasing orchids across the globe.

"You say you care about me," she continued, "but if you really did, you wouldn't ask me to give up everything I've built." The honesty in her words seemed to dig deep into the soil of their past, unearthing the truth they both knew but had never faced.

Scott looked down, then back up at her with a vulnerability that was rare for him to show. "You're right," he admitted, his voice barely louder than the rustle of leaves in the gentle night breeze. "I just... I haven't given up on us, Alice. Not yet."

She met his gaze. "Goodbye, Scott." The words were not harsh, but they held the finality of autumn's last leaf falling to the ground.

"Goodbye, Alice."

It didn't feel right to let him go without telling him what she'd discovered tonight. "Before you leave, you might want to look into Lucille Girard."

"Girard? Why?" He looked up, clearly confused.

She bit her lip. "I'd rather not say more. Just . . . trust me, okay?"

"Okay, Alice. I'll check her out. Remember, if you change your mind, I'm only a phone call away." With those words, he turned and walked away, his figure gradually disappearing into the shadows of the garden, leaving Alice alone with the comforting embrace of her familiar surroundings.

CHAPTER NINETEEN

Alice woke to the cheerful chirping of birds and soft morning light filtering through the lace curtains. She'd slept well. What she'd said to Scott had been as much for her benefit as his. Putting her feelings into words made them feel more solid.

She stretched, her muscles still feeling the previous day's work in the estate's sprawling gardens. It was a good kind of hurt, though, one brought on by honest labor and time with her hands in the dirt. With a contented sigh, she swung her legs over the edge of the bed and decided today was a new day—a day to re-focus on the garden project that brought her to this French estate in the first place. It wasn't her job to figure out who had killed René DuPont. While Inspector Fournier might be suspicious of her and Marco, he wouldn't find any evidence of wrongdoing from either of them because they were both innocent.

She wasn't naïve. She knew innocent people had been charged and even convicted of crimes. She just didn't think Fournier had it in for the two of them so completely that he would ignore facts.

Still, as she combed her fingers through her hair, her thoughts drifted to the list of suspects she had been mulling over the past few days. One by one, she mentally crossed off the names of those who could not have been involved in René's untimely death. Lambert had an alibi. Girard had no reason to kill DuPont. Marco vouched for Claire LeBlanc and, if she was to believed, she didn't have a motive. And now, with no one left to suspect, Alice felt an odd mixture of relief and frustration. The mystery seemed to be at a standstill.

For all she knew, René had mistaken the hemlock for something else and had poisoned himself. "Poisoned by a simple mistake," she murmured to herself, a mix of sadness and scientific fascination in her voice. It would be a tragic irony if his own misplaced confidence in his knowledge of flora had led to his demise.There might be no murder at all. Surely, Inspector Fournier would figure that out soon enough if it were the case.

She headed downstairs, determined to channel her restless energy into reviving the cottage gardens. Stepping outside, Alice breathed in the fresh morning air laced with the subtle scent of roses and earth and looked around. What would she tackle today?

Frowning at the spot where the hydrangeas used to be, she stuck the toe of her clog in the soil. Who had poisoned the soil and why? That was still a mystery, too. What if whoever it was came back to ruin other parts of the garden? But like the question of who killed René, she had no suspects. She couldn't think of anyone who would have benefitted from killing those innocent plants.

Alice knocked the soil off her shoes. There was work to be done, and though the shadow of the investigation loomed, the gardens—and her passion for them—beckoned her forward.

But first, breakfast. She went into the kitchen. Only Marco was there. "Morning," she said.

As an answer, he set a cup of café au last in front of her.

Alice scooped a spoonful of Marco's homemade granola, the crunch of oats and nuts mingling with the sweet burst of dried berries. As she chewed, Marco cleared his throat from across the rustic kitchen table.

"About last night," he began, his voice tinged with hesitation, "I didn't mean to, but I overheard your chat with Scott."

She set her spoon down, looking deeply into his earnest brown ones. The morning sun streamed through the window, casting a warm glow on his face and highlighting the apology etched in his features.

"Marco, you don't have to—"

"No, I need to say this." He leaned forward, hands clasped. "I was jealous, and it was wrong to eavesdrop. But, Alice," he paused, choosing his words carefully, "your strength amazes me. The way you stand so firmly on your own—it's one of the things I admire most about you."

Her cheeks warmed at his words. To be recognized for her independence meant more than any compliment on her designs or her looks. It confirmed that Marco saw her as Alice Bloom, the woman who cultivated beauty from the soil, not just an extension of him or a prize to be won.

"Thank you, Marco," Alice replied, her voice soft but steady. "That means a lot to me."

A comfortable silence settled between them as they finished their breakfast, each lost in their own thoughts. When the last bite was taken, Alice rose and rinsed her bowl, her mind already transitioning back to the garden and her plans for it. "Do you know where Sophie is?"

"I think she said she was going to be out in the vineyard this morning and then back in the winery this afternoon," Marco said.

She turned to leave, but he grabbed her hand. "Alice, I hate this tension between us. I've never felt what I feel about you with anyone else. I don't want to spoil it. I'm sorry I didn't tell you about Claire sooner. I should have."

She looked down at her small hand in his big one, both of them roughened by the work they did. "I feel the same way, Marco. Without trust, though, I'm not sure where this can go."

He bowed his head. "I understand." Then he looked up at her. "I will show you that you can trust me." Then he lifted her hand to his lips and kissed the knuckles. "Go out and have a beautiful day in your garden."

Alice strolled out toward the orderly marching lines of the grapevines, her hands jammed deep in her overall pockets. She could see Sophie in the distance and made her way toward her. The assistant vintner looked up as Alice approached, her expression smoothing into a smile.

Alice felt her face forming a smile in return. She liked Sophie. It was good to make a friend. One of the reasons Alice had been so glad to see Marco when he'd arrived was it meant she wouldn't be so lonely on this job. Now, however, feeling like there was a barrier between them made her feel even more lonely than she would have been if he'd never come. Having someone like Sophie to connect with lessened the sting of that, too.

"Morning, Alice. How may I assist you?" Sophie asked as Alice reached her.

"It's those pesky hydrangeas," Alice said, getting straight to the point. "I want to be sure I know what's really in that soil. I want to be sure it's not going to impact any other areas of the garden. Any chance we could run some tests on it in your lab?"

"Of course," Sophie agreed without hesitation. "Give me a few more minutes here, then I'll meet you in the lab."

Alice made her way back down to the winery and its gleaming lab. True to her word, Sophie arrived a few minutes later. Together, they gathered the necessary equipment and made their way to the area in question.

"Let's start here," Alice instructed, gesturing to the center of the small plot.

"Absolutely," Sophie concurred, kneeling beside her and plunging a trowel into the earth.

Alice scooped a handful of soil, letting the dark loam crumble between her fingers as she examined its texture. Beside her, Sophie methodically filled test tubes, labeling each with meticulous care. The scent of damp earth mingled with the faint perfume of lavender and rose—a blend that spoke of life and decay in one breath.

They worked in tandem, collecting samples with efficiency and care. Alice smiled. It was good to work with someone who shared her approach to plants. She loved their beauty, but she also loved the science beneath them. Sophie clearly had the same approach. Alice felt hers showed in the gardens and she knew Sophie's showed in the quality of the wine she made.

"Your investigation," Sophie began, breaking the rhythm of their task. "Any progress?"

Alice paused, sitting back on her heels before responding. "I'm thinking it might be time to let it go. Oddly enough, I have this hunch that René may have mistaken hemlock for something edible. A tragic, self-inflicted mistake."

Sophie's expression turned contemplative, a wrinkle appearing on her forehead as she capped a vial. "That's so like him. René had an unfortunate tendency to overestimate his own expertise. Never asked for help. Overrode assistance if it pleased him. If it was his arrogance that did him in... well, that's rather poetic justice, isn't it?"

"Perhaps," Alice mused, not entirely convinced but finding a strange comfort in the idea. Their hands resumed their work, the motion almost meditative as they sifted through the garden's secrets, searching for answers in the very soil that nurtured life and witnessed death.

Overhead, the sky, which had been a clear expanse of blue all morning, began to sully with bruise-like smudges. A hush fell over the garden as if nature itself held its breath. She glanced up, noting the ominous change.

"Looks like a storm's brewing," Sophie commented, squinting towards the gathering clouds. Her voice held a note of concern, but her movements remained precise and unhurried as she sealed another vial.

"Those dark clouds are rolling in quicker than I expected," Alice agreed, standing up and brushing dirt from her knees. She could feel the shift in the air, the static charge of an impending downpour.

"Let's pack up. We should get these samples inside before we're caught in it," Sophie said, now urgency lacing her words.

They moved with efficiency, collecting their equipment. Just as they secured the last of the test tubes in the portable carrier, the wind picked up, sending a chill through the air and leaves skittering across the path.

"Come on," Alice urged, gripping the handle of the carrier firmly. Together, they hurried towards the lab, the first heavy drops of rain beginning to fall, pattering against the broad leaves around them like a prelude to the storm's symphony.

"Almost there," Sophie called out, just ahead, as she pushed open the door to the sanctuary of the lab. They slipped inside, and not a moment too soon—just as the door clicked shut behind them than the rain erupted into a torrential cascade, drumming fiercely against the windows.

"Safe and sound," Alice declared with a relieved smile, setting down their precious cargo of soil samples on the workbench. Outside, the world turned a silvery-grey, the garden transformed by the deluge, but inside, the steady beat of rain against the roof only seemed to underscore the warmth and security of the lab.

CHAPTER TWENTY

Alice delicately pinched a sample of soil between her fingers, feeling its texture as she searched for clues within its composition. Beside her, Sophie was already peering through the eyepiece of a microscope, her focus fixed on the minuscule world contained in a single drop of water mixed with earth.

"Anything?" Alice asked, not sure what she hoped to find in the samples they'd taken.

"Traces of pyrethrin," Sophie replied without looking up, "It's an organic pesticide. Not what you'd typically find here."

"Are there any organic winemakers nearby who might use it?" Alice's curiosity was piqued. It was an odd thing to find in just one area of the garden.

"Actually, yes." Sophie straightened up. "Henri Rousseau. He's quite the evangelist for the natural wine movement around these parts."

"Natural wine movement? All wine seems pretty natural to me." Alice sat down on one of the rolling stools in the lab. The name rang a bell. Where had she heard it before?

Sophie laughed. "I suppose it does, but the natural wine movement takes it a bit further. They're all about sustainability and terroir. You know, the whole idea that a particular region produces unique characteristics that impart a certain flavor and aroma. The less interference with synthetic chemicals and processing, the better for both the wine and the land."

"Interesting," Alice said. "But how's the wine?"

"Uneven, to be honest, but that's on purpose. They try to service the grapes rather than making the grapes service them. Each harvest might yield something a little different, and they want the wine to reflect that." Sophie leaned back against the lab bench and crossed one foot over the other.

"And Henri Rousseau's wine?" Alice asked.

Sophie shrugged. "Some of it's great. Some of it, not so much."

"How did René feel about the whole movement and about Henri?" Alice asked. René had seemed a little old-fashioned.

"He wasn't too fond of the man's methods—or his product." She straightened and began to clean up the lab bench. "He wasn't quiet about it, either."

"Really?" Alice arched an eyebrow. Now she remembered. Henri Rousseau was one of the names René had mentioned on her first day here. Something about not giving René his due respect?

"At the annual local winemakers' dinner, René made no effort to hide his disdain. He said Rousseau's wines tasted like vinegar," Sophie confided, her lips curling into a wry smile. "It was quite the talk of the town. Rousseau threatened to punch him in the nose and had to be held back by several waiters. Everyone asked and shook their heads, but it was probably the most exciting thing that had happened at that dinner in decades. I think they secretly loved the drama."

Alice nodded slowly, taking in the new information. It sounded like it was René who hadn't given Rousseau his due respect. Maybe her investigation wasn't so dead after all. Before she could ask more questions, though, a delivery van pulled up, and a man hopped out to unload boxes emblazoned with the logo of the estate, moving quickly to avoid getting too wet. Sophie excused herself and went over to sign off on the delivery.

"New labels?" Alice called out, her eyes following Sophie as she inspected a sheet pulled from one of the boxes.

"Yes, for the rosé," Sophie said, holding up the label for Alice to see. The design was delicate, imbued with hues of pink and gold that captured the essence of the setting sun. "Soleil Mignon," she read aloud, a touch of pride lighting up her voice.

"Pretty sun," Alice translated, smiling at how the name danced on her tongue. Then she frowned. "René's mother is out of the picture then?"

"Just her first name. It's still a Château DuPont product," Sophie sat down on one of the nearby stools. "And it was her notes on best practices to make a rosé that inspired my approach to making Soleil Mignon."

"Really?" Alice took a seat next to her. "I didn't know that."

Sophie reached behind her and pulled out a battered journal. Setting it down in front of Alice, she said, "I'm not sure anyone did. I tried to tell René about it, but he wasn't much interested."

Alice picked up the journal, the outside of it embroidered with vining roses. "I'm surprised. He seemed to really venerate his mother."

Sophie shrugged. "René seemed like a lot of things to a lot of people. Sometimes the reality was quite different. Plus, Jeannette never

115

named anything after herself. I'm not sure she'd have liked that. Naming this wine after one person never felt quite right to me, either. This rosé is so special. I wanted something that reflected that. Something that spoke of romance, of Provence itself, more than just heritage."

Alice couldn't help but admire the label. It was a bold move, harnessing the allure of the region rather than the sentimentality of family. But then again, if anyone knew how to blend the traditional with the innovative, it was Sophie.

Hefting the last of the boxes stacked beside the door, Alice followed Sophie into the cool expanse of the storage room. The scent of oak barrels and fermenting grapes mingled with the earthy aroma of the countryside, a fragrance that always made Alice feel more at home.

"Look at this," she said, placing the box on a sturdy wooden table and pointing to the labels again. "Soleil Mignon. Those are actually your initials, aren't they?"

Sophie glanced back with a start, a look of surprise flickering in her eyes before she laughed softly. "I hadn't noticed when I came up with the name. How funny."

"Serendipity," Alice mused, smiling as she imagined the labels gracing bottles across Provence, each one carrying a secret signature of their creator. "Maybe it's a sign."

"Let's hope it's a good one." Sophie slid the box into its designated slot, eyeing the stacks with satisfaction.

"Say, Sophie," Alice began, pausing near the window that overlooked rows of lush vines drinking up the spring rain, "would you be able to arrange a visit to Rousseau's vineyard for me? I could feign interest in sourcing some organic plants for a new project." It wouldn't be a complete fabrication. She was interested in Rousseau's techniques and how they worked.

Sophie turned to face Alice with a furrowed brow. "I thought you had put aside your sleuthing hat. The police are all over the case now, aren't they?"

"I'm not sure how all over it they are," Alice said, tracing a line in the condensation on the glass. Her curiosity, however, was far from quenched. "This one last lead—it might just tie everything together."

Sophie examined Alice. After a moment, she offered a nod, albeit a reluctant one. "All right, I'll see what I can do. Henri is a bit reclusive, but I think he'll be open to discussing his passion for organic viticulture."

"Thank you, Sophie." Alice allowed herself a small smile, the prospect of uncovering the truth propelling her forward. She didn't know what awaited her at Rousseau's vineyard, but each step felt like a stride closer to solving the puzzle of René Dupont's untimely demise.

Alice watched Sophie's fingers dance over the delicate labels of the new rosé, arranging them with a precision that spoke of years tending to the finer details of winemaking. The scent of lavender and vineyard soil mingled in the cool air of the cellar, grounding her thoughts as they veered towards the upcoming encounter.

"Look," Sophie began, breaking the silence, "I know you're chasing down leads, but Henri Rousseau? He's practically a walking embodiment of the Summer of Love. I can't imagine him so much as squashing a grape too harshly, let alone..."

"Resorting to murder?" Alice completed Sophie's thought, her eyebrows arching in gentle inquiry. She had seen enough of life's unexpected turns to keep an open mind.

"Exactly," said Sophie, nodding emphatically. "He's all about harmony and balance. His philosophy is to create wine that's in peaceful co-existence with the earth—not disrupting it. It's hard to picture someone like that orchestrating René's death."

"Philosophies can be complex," Alice countered softly, her gaze steady on Sophie. "People, even more so. But I appreciate your insight. Still, I'd like to meet him. Get a sense of the man behind the ethos."

Sophie exhaled slowly. "All right," she finally conceded, "I'll set it up. You can talk plants and biodynamics all you want. Just don't expect to find a cold-blooded killer pruning his vines."

"Thanks, Sophie." Alice's voice was laced with sincerity. "I promise to tread lightly. Who knows, maybe all I'll find are some tips for my next sustainable garden design."

"Maybe," Sophie echoed, her smile not quite reaching her eyes as she turned back to the labels. The name Soleil Mignon gleamed under the cellar lights.

Alice left the lab and went back to the garden. The rain had stopped, and the scent of blooming lavender hung in the air, a soothing balm to the tension that had wound itself into her muscles. She smiled the conditions were perfect for planting. She gathered her tools and went to work.

When she was done, she followed the path she'd planned that snaked through the garden, rather than rigidly creating right angles. She stopped at a bed of heirloom roses, their petals a delicate ballet of pinks and creams iridescent as the sun hit the waterdrops still adorning them. She really wanted to honor René's desire to plant more hydrangeas in the garden, but roses were so much more able to handle an acidic soil.

She wondered if René's mother had planted these very roses. Given the variety and how well established they were, it certainly was possible. She should take a closer look at Jeannette's portrait in the sitting room to see what roses surrounded her in the painting. Strange that there should be so much about Jeannette that connected to roses like the portrait and her recipe for rose petal jam and the embroidered roses on the outside of her journal when René said her favorite flower was hydrangea.

Perhaps René had it wrong and it was roses that Jeannette DuPont had loved and not hydrangeas at all? Claire LeBlanc had made it sound like René and his mother hadn't been close, and Sophie certainly had hinted at that as well. Perhaps it would be okay to pull out the hydrangeas and make that spot into one of the little seating areas rather than trying to save that particular batch of soil. Maybe if she didn't plant more hydrangeas, whoever had sabotaged what was there wouldn't be tempted to create more mischief.

Alice headed towards the main house. The stone façade rose before her, vines climbing up its sides like nature's own embroidery. Despite the undercurrent of mystery that seemed to permeate the estate, the château retained an undeniable charm.

As she reached the ornate front door, Alice noticed an envelope protruding from the mail slot, an incongruous sight against the old-world elegance of the heavy oak. With a frown, she extracted the folded paper, noting its lack of postage or markings. A chill prickled her skin despite the warmth of the late afternoon sun.

Turning the envelope over in her hands, she found it unsealed. Inside was a single sheet of plain stationery, the message upon it typed in an impersonal font that did nothing to soften the stark warning:

"Ms. Bloom, consider this a friendly piece of advice. Your digging has not gone unnoticed. Back off your investigation before you get hurt. This is your last warning."

The words seemed to leap off the page, casting long shadows across Alice's thoughts. She scanned the courtyard, half-expecting to catch the eye of someone lurking in the shadows, watching. But there was only the gentle rustling of leaves and the distant call of a songbird.

For a moment, Alice stood statue-still, letting the implications of the message sink in. Someone was taking her inquiries seriously, seriously enough to threaten her safety. A surge of defiance swelled within her chest. She had come to this idyllic corner of Provence to work in the simplicity of soil and vine, but instead, she had unearthed a tangle of secrets.

Tucking the letter into her jacket pocket, Alice lifted her chin with resolve. Whoever penned this note had underestimated her tenacity, her drive to see things through to their root. Threats be damned, she would not be so easily deterred.

With a renewed sense of purpose, she made her way into the château, the click of the latch echoing in the quiet hall as she closed the door behind her. Tomorrow, she would visit Rousseau's vineyard, and perhaps there, amidst the organic vines, she would find a clue that would help unravel the tightly knotted mystery that had taken hold of Château DuPont.

CHAPTER TWENTY ONE

After lunch, the rain began again and was coming down too hard to do much planting. Alice went up to her room to do some thinking about her garden plans. There were already so many beautiful examples of vintage roses in the garden, she could see making it into a theme. They were a little more water-intensive than she liked, but there were some that were more drought tolerant.

She shut her eyes and leaned back in her chair, thinking about what she might plant. Wait! She had it! Perle d'or! Golden Pearl in French. It was another heirloom variety, so it would fit in with the Fantin de Latours that were already here. The sweet round apricot blooms would look wonderful in the dappled shade around that spot where the hydrangeas had been. Now, to see if she could actually get some!

Her cell phone buzzed with a text. She took it out and frowned at the unfamiliar number, but opened it.

Bon jour, Mademoiselle Bloom. This is Henri Rousseau. Mademoiselle Moreau has told me you wish to know more about natural winemaking and the organic processes I use. I am free this evening, if you would care to meet me at my vineyard.

Alice looked out the window where the rain had begun again. Not exactly great vineyard touring weather. She replied:

Merci, Monsieur Rousseau. I would love to see the vineyard if the weather breaks tonight. I will text you at this number when I leave Château DuPont.

The reply came instantly:

Magnifique. A bientôt.

She made a note about her Perle d'Or thought and headed downstairs in search of Jean-Baptiste to see if he would be available to drive her that evening. The kitchen was empty, although it smelled amazing. Grabbing an umbrella from a stand by the back door, she went first to the garage. Empty. Then the winery where Sophie said she hadn't seen him. Finally back to the house. Finding Lilou in René's office, she knocked lightly on the open door.

"Seen Jean-Baptiste around?" Alice asked. "I was hoping he might be able to give me a ride later."

Lilou looked up from the paperwork she'd been frowning at. "It's his day off. I expect he's gone to town to spend some time with his friends there. Would you like me to call him to see if he'd come back early?"

"Absolutely not," Alice said. She bit her lip. She could follow a map and it wasn't like the French drove on the wrong side of the road. She could handle driving a few miles herself. "Would you mind if I borrowed a car?"

"Of course not," Lilou responded, waving a dismissive hand. "The keys should be hanging in the kitchen."

"Thanks." She went back to the kitchen. This time Marco was there, stirring something in the Dutch oven on the stove. "What's for dinner tonight?"

"A daube." He looked up from the pot. "It needs to cook for a little while longer."

"What's a daube?" she asked as she found the key rack and pulled the one for the car Jean-Baptiste had been using to drive her around.

"Another classic Provencal dish. Kind of like a beef stew." He put the lid back on the pot. "Are you going somewhere?"

"Possibly. I have some new gardening techniques to learn." She'd keep the part about following a lead to herself for now. No need to get everyone stirred up before she knew if Rousseau could possibly be involved.

"In the rain?" Marco made a face.

Alice laughed. "I'm hoping the rain stops before it's time to go. It has until this evening."

Heading upstairs, she realized she was hoping the rain stopped and that she could learn a few things from Henri Rousseau about natural wine and his techniques. It would be a fruitful excursion even if it didn't move her murder investigation forward.

***

Just before the sun began to set, the clouds parted and the rain stopped. Alice texted Rousseau to say she was on her way. He texted back to tell her where on his property to meet him. The area was large, and the directions were a little circuitous. She hoped they would make more sense once she was there. She didn't want to delay her arrival. She wouldn't be able to stay long. It would be dark soon.

She drove through the wine country, with rows upon rows of vines unfurling like green ribbons beside her. She nearly missed the turn onto

Rousseau's property. It wasn't marked, and it looked like hardly more than a path. She eased the car along, her gaze tracing the well-tended rows of grapevines that stretched across Rousseau's estate. The sky had cleared just enough for a pale wash of sunset to brush the clouds, painting the world in hues of rose and gold. She parked near a stile that led over a split rail fence. The vines began their ascent up the hill on the other side.

Snapping open her umbrella as the first drops of rain began to fall again, Alice stepped onto the damp earth. Her boots sinking slightly into the wet ground. The air was rich with the scent of damp soil and growing things. Following Rousseau's directions, she walked along the edge of the vineyard, her eyes drinking in the verdant landscape as the hill stole her breath with its steep incline.

She reached the designated meeting spot—an old oak tree that stood sentinel over the vines. Its ancient limbs bore witness to countless seasons, and now it waited, as did Alice, but there was no sign of Henri Rousseau.

Leaning against the trunk, she let her gaze wander over the carefully pruned grapevines. Rain spattered the leaves. They looked beautiful and healthy. Each plant was a testament to Rousseau's techniques and care. The shoots were trained with precision, and the ground beneath was free of weeds—a labor of love that spoke directly to Alice's horticulturist heart.

As the rain gathered strength, tapping a rhythm on her umbrella, Alice felt a shiver tickle the back of her neck, then she heard something rustling. She glanced around the empty expanse of the vineyard, expecting to see Rousseau making his way to her, but seeing nothing. There was something unsettling about the solitude, the way the vines seemed to watch her with their clustered eyes.

"Stop it, Alice," she scolded herself, wrapping her arms tightly around her torso. "It's just that nasty letter playing tricks on you." The anonymous warning she'd received earlier had been brief but unsettling enough to seed doubt and suspicion where there had been none. Someone thought she knew more than she did, or she was closer to the solution than she realized.

Calm yourself. Make a list. Plants that look like they have eyes. Actaea pachypoda. Ochna serrulata. Acmella oleracea. Mimulus. Anemone coronaria.

Another loud rustling noise startled her. "Probably just a rabbit or a curious bird." She forced a laugh to break the tension that clung to her like the dampness in the air, but she couldn't deny the unease that settled heavily in her stomach. She had a strange sense that she was not alone in the twilight of Rousseau's vineyards and that whoever was there didn't wish her well.

Alice checked her watch again, the minute hand creeping past the agreed time with a sluggish indifference. Thirty minutes late. Her fingers danced over the smartphone's screen, seeking Henri Rousseau's contact to send him a quick message. The device, usually so brimming with bars of connectivity, now displayed a mocking 'No Service' at the top corner.

With a shake of her head, she tucked the uncooperative phone back into her pocket. She glanced up at the sky, where dark clouds had started to knit together, a gray tapestry that promised more than a gentle shower. The droplets pattered against her umbrella in an increasingly aggressive tempo—a warning siren from nature itself.

"Okay, Alice, time to call it a night," she decided, her voice small against the rising wind. It wasn't just the worsening weather urging her departure; there was an undeniable feeling of danger. Henri's absence gnawed at her, an unanswered question that seemed to hang heavy on the vine-laden branches around her. Had something happened to him to keep him from meeting her? Did he have information that would help her figure out what had happened to René and why? She'd contact him again when she got back to the château and see if they could reschedule.

With one last look at the empty meeting spot, Alice turned and began her descent down the hill. The raindrops grew larger, insistent, as if hurrying her along. Then, without a herald, the sky split open with a bright flash, and a crack of thunder roared across the vineyard.

She flinched, the sound reverberating through her chest, and her grip on the umbrella handle tightened. The realization dawned on her— she was exposed on this elevated ground, a lone figure attracting the very elements she sought to escape. Her heart hammered a frantic beat, mirroring the staccato of rain on fabric.

Make a list. Plants that like a lot of rain. Lobelia cardinalis. Thalictrum dasycarpum. Heuchera sanguinea.

Quickening her pace while the rational part of her mind was occupied with making lists, she hurried toward where she'd left the car. Lightning flashed again, closer this time, followed by a boom that seemed to roll through the rows of grapevines. Each vine now seemed like a specter in the dance of light and shadow.

"Come on, Alice, just a little further," she encouraged herself. The romantic allure of the vineyard at sunset had been wholly replaced by a primal urge for shelter, warmth, and safety—a stark reminder that even in pursuit of passion, nature remained an unpredictable force to be respected.

Alice squinted at the blurred outline of her car in the distance, the umbrella doing little to shield her from the tempest's wrath. She focused on the rhythm of her footsteps, trying to outpace the storm's fury as the mud sucked at her boots with each hurried step.

"Almost there," she murmured, willing her legs to move faster over the uneven terrain of Rousseau's vineyard.

Suddenly, her foot caught on something concealed beneath the watery veil that had transformed the ground. An irrigation line, hidden like a serpent in the grass, sent her sprawling forward with a cry. Pain lanced through her ankle as it twisted beneath her, and for a moment, Alice lay still, staring up at the sky, rain pummeling her.

"Get up, Alice," she commanded herself, her voice barely a whisper above the storm's din. With gritted teeth, she pushed herself up, testing her weight on the injured ankle. A sharp jolt of pain shot up her leg, and she stifled a whimper. She was already soaked, so she closed the umbrella and used it as a cane. Hobbling, she resumed her journey to the car, each step an agony.

Plants that can relieve pain. Tabernaemontana divaricate. Euphorbia resinfera. Lactuca virosa.

The world seemed to shrink to the throb of her ankle and the relentless drumming of raindrops. The rows of grapevines swayed menacingly, their earlier charm lost to the gloom. She could almost imagine them reaching out, grasping at her, as if animated by the same malice that had drawn her here under false pretenses.

Finally reaching the stile, she climbed over, trying not to put any more weight on her ankle than she absolutely had to. Only a few more yards. Alice fumbled for the keys, shivering as the cold rain plastered her clothes to her body. Something was wrong with the car, though. It tilted at a strange angle. Her fingers brushed the rubber of the front tire, and her heart sank. It wasn't just flat—it was shredded, the work unmistakably deliberate. A surge of fear washed through her as she checked the other tires, finding them in the same condition.

"Who would do this?" she gasped, peering into the encroaching darkness. Was it someone who wanted to frighten her away from the case? Could it be the same person who sent the letter? Or someone who wanted to strand her out here in the storm? Someone who truly wished her harm?

Rain streamed down her face, mixing with the unease that settled in her stomach. The thought that someone might be watching made her skin crawl. Alone, with no phone signal and now no transportation, the danger of her situation pressed in on her like the storm clouds above.

"Think, Alice," she said aloud, forcing herself to take slow, measured breaths despite the panic that clawed at her composure. "There has to be a way out of this."

But as lightning split the sky once more, illuminating the desolation of the vineyard around her, Alice couldn't shake the feeling that she was trapped in a game designed by an opponent who was always one step ahead.

Alice pressed her back against the side of the car, using it as a shield from the relentless wind that whipped through the vineyard. The rain had transformed the ground to mud, slippery and treacherous underfoot, making every step an effort. She scanned the horizon, but the rows of vines offered no direction, no hint of sanctuary.

"Come on," she muttered, rallying herself. A landscape designer by trade, she understood the lay of the land better than most. She tried to remember the route she had taken earlier when the skies had been clear. There had been a farmhouse, hadn't there? A light somewhere in the distance.

With her ankle throbbing, Alice wrapped her arms tightly around her torso, trying to preserve what little warmth she had left. She took a hesitant step forward, wincing at the pain. Thunder rumbled, a low growl that rolled over the hills, and she couldn't help but flinch.

"Focus on what you know," she coached herself. Plants needed water, sun, and soil to thrive. And people? People needed shelter, safety, connection. Right now, she was as isolated as one could get.

The eerie feeling of being watched crept up on her again. She cast a nervous glance over her shoulder, half expecting to see a shadow detach itself from the rows of vines. But there was nothing—only the ominous flutter of leaves and the occasional flash of lightning that tore across the sky, exposing the starkness of her solitude.

Her mind turned to Jazz, her best friend who could always be counted on for a laugh or a lifeline. But Jazz was miles away, nestled in the cozy warmth of her tea shop. Daisy would be beside herself if she knew the peril her sister was in. She couldn't even call to tell them about it and get their encouragement. Her phone still had no signal.

A gust of wind nearly toppled her, and Alice realized that standing still was not an option. She had to move, had to try something, anything. She steadied herself and began to hobble along the path that led down the hill, each step an act of will.

"Get to the road," she whispered, a mantra to keep the creeping dread at bay. "You'll be able to call for help there."

But as the night deepened and the storm raged on, the road seemed farther and farther away. Alice found herself praying for rescue in a vast expanse of cultivated wilderness—a place where even her considerable knowledge of botany seemed as insignificant as a single drop in the rain-soaked soil.

CHAPTER TWENTY TWO

Alice limped along the pitted muddy track, her ankle a twisted agony with each step. With each gust of wind, the storm seemed to laugh at her plight, pelting her with rain that stung like needles against her skin. Hunger gnawed at her insides, a constant reminder of the dinner she had missed back at the château. But survival eclipsed comfort, and the road promised a chance at a signal, a lifeline to call for help.

She clutched her hair into a makeshift bun, attempting to shield her eyes from the relentless downpour. Her phone, secured in the pocket of her waterproof jacket, was a useless brick still without reception. Each breath came in ragged gasps, and her mind whirled with thoughts of warm food and dry clothes. Yet, Alice pushed on, driven by the same determination that led her through countless gardens, sculpting nature into art.

Suddenly, the darkness ahead fractured, split by the advancing glow of headlights. Hope surged through her, as vibrant as the first sprout in springtime. She stumbled toward the roadside, wincing at the sharp pain radiating up from her ankle. Mustering every ounce of strength, she waved her arms overhead, desperate to catch the driver's attention.

"Over here!" she shouted, though her voice was snatched away by the wind. The lights drew nearer, twin beacons in the tempestuous night. Alice stood there, a solitary figure against the elements, her spirit unyielding, waiting for salvation to arrive on wheels.

The truck's engine rumbled to a stop, and the door swung open. Marco got out, his broad-shouldered silhouette framed against the truck's headlights. Without hesitation, he strode towards her, the mud splashing beneath his boots, his face etched with concern beneath the brim of a soaked baseball cap. "Alice! What happened? Are you all right?"

"Marco!" Alice fell into his arms , relief washing over her like the rain that drenched her to the bone. "Thank goodness."

He held her against his chest for a moment. "Let's get you into the truck."

She took one step and let out a small cry of pain. "I twisted my ankle. It's hard to walk."

He swooped her up into his arms and carried her. Once they were both inside the truck, a little bubble of dry warmth in the storm, he said, "I was worried when you didn't make it back for dinner. I couldn't reach you by phone." Marco retrieved a thick blanket from behind the seat and wrapped it around her.

"Thanks," she murmured, her teeth chattering. She pulled the blanket tighter, the warmth seeping slowly into her chilled bones. She managed a weak smile, warmed by more than just the blanket. Marco put the truck in gear, and they started back toward the road.

"How did you find me?" she asked. She'd barely found where to enter the property, and she had directions from the owner.

"The car has GPS," Marco said, keeping his eyes on the path in front of them.

She frowned. "My phone had no service. I would think the car would be out of range, too."

"It was," he confirmed. "But I could see its last known location. I drove there and saw the path with recent tire tracks on it."

"Smart," she said. In her head, she added kind and talented and handsome. The windshield wipers beat a steady rhythm against the deluge as Marco navigated the work truck through the slippery backroads leading to the château. Alice sat huddled in the passenger seat, the blanket cocooning her from the chill that still lingered on her skin.

"Marco," she said, her voice steadier now, "I can't believe you came out looking for me in this weather." She turned to him, her eyes reflecting the gratitude that swelled within her chest.

He glanced at her, his hands firmly on the wheel. "Of course I did," he replied, the edges of his mouth turning up in a gentle smile. "My only regret is not coming with you from the start. You shouldn't be going out alone. Not with the threats that have been made against you."

Alice felt a warmth spread through her that had nothing to do with the heater blasting at their feet. His concern was like a balm to the unease that still clung to her thoughts.

"What happened?" he asked.

"Rousseau sent me a text saying he'd meet me this evening," she began, hesitating as the memory of the afternoon's events surfaced. "But when I got there, he wasn't around."

"Wasn't around?" Marco echoed, his brow furrowing beneath the rearview mirror's reflection.

"Exactly," Alice continued, twisting the blanket in her fingers.

"And the longer I waited, the more it felt like...like someone was watching me." Her gaze drifted to the rain-streaked window, the shadows between the vines playing back in her mind.

"That doesn't sound good." Concern laced his tone. He reached over, giving her hand a reassuring squeeze before returning it to the steering wheel.

"No, it doesn't," Alice agreed, her mind racing with possibilities. She leaned back into the seat, the fabric of the blanket soft against her cheek. Despite the lingering fear and confusion, she couldn't help but feel a measure of safety. With Marco beside her, the storm outside seemed a little less threatening. "It didn't feel good, either."

"Are you certain the message was from Rousseau?" Marco asked, his voice carrying over the sound of the rain pelting against the truck's exterior.

Alice furrowed her brow, "Who else would it be from?" She grimaced, the dull throb in her ankle a stark reminder of the afternoon's folly.

"Someone who wanted you alone and vulnerable." Marco navigated the truck around a bend, the headlights cutting through the veil of darkness and rain. "It's just that anyone with a bit of tech savvy could fake a number, make it seem like the text was coming from someone else."

"Fake it?" Alice considered this new angle, the implications sending a shiver down her spine that wasn't solely from the cold.

"Unfortunately, it's quite easy," Marco replied, his voice steady despite the concern etching his features. "But let's not worry about that now. We're almost home."

True to his word, the welcoming lights of the château soon pierced the night, a beacon of warmth and safety. They pulled up to the entrance, and Marco was quick to assist Alice out of the truck, supporting her as they made their way inside.

"Alice! What happened? Are you all right?" Lilou rushed to her.

"Wet and a little lame." Alice pointed to her ankle.

"You stay right here. I'll go up to your room and get you some dry clothes."

"Thank you, Lilou." The thought of having to climb the stairs didn't appeal.

In a flash, Lilou was back with yoga pants and a long-sleeved t-shirt. "Come. You can change in the office."

She peeled off the layers of damp clothes and changed into the dry clothes. Lilou snatched the pile of wet clothes and whisked them off to the laundry room. The comfort of warm, dry fabric against Alice's skin felt like an embrace, a contrast to the chaos of the storm outside.

Returning to the kitchen, the savory aroma of daube filled the air, enveloping her in the rich tapestry of herbs and spices that Marco was known for. He plated a generous portion over egg noodles and set it in front of her, while Lilou, ever the mother hen, hovered close by, adjusting the blanket around Alice's shoulders.

"Here, eat this. It'll warm you up," Marco encouraged, his eyes reflecting the flickering light of the hearth.

"Thanks," Alice murmured, gratefully accepting the steaming dish. The flavors of tender beef, red wine, and herbs danced on her tongue. In that moment, with the storm's rage reduced to a mere background whisper, Alice allowed herself the luxury of feeling cared for, the earlier fears momentarily forgotten in the simple joy of a shared meal.

The kitchen door swung open with a gust of wind, and Sophie stomped in, shedding water from her heavy rain poncho like a dog after a bath. Her boots left muddy imprints on the stone tiles as she peeled off the layers of waterproof fabric.

"French drains are clear," she announced, hanging her poncho on a hook by the door to drip dry. "Grapes are safe for now." Despite the roughness of the storm outside, her tone carried the satisfaction of a job well done, her dedication to the vineyard evident even under the worst weather conditions.

Alice watched her, appreciating Sophie's diligence. It was the same care and attention she put into her own landscape designs, understanding how crucial it is to protect the fruits of one's labor against nature's unpredictable moods.

Sophie turned to Alice and started. "What happened to you?"

Alice told her story once again.

"You're sure the tires were slashed? That they aren't just flat?" Sophie asked, brows furrowed. "It must have been hard to see in the dark and the rain."

"I suppose they could have been flat, but it really felt like they'd been tampered with," Alice said.

"We'll have to take a look tomorrow once the storm passes." Sophie crossed over to the stove and put the kettle on. "Anyone else want tea?"

After chatting a few minutes more about the vineyard and the close call with the storm, Marco glanced at the old grandfather clock against the wall. "We should get you upstairs, Alice. You must be tired."

Alice agreed, feeling the exhaustion from the day's events weighing on her. She leaned on Marco as they left the kitchen, , her steps slow, favoring her injured ankle.

They ascended the staircase slowly, one careful step at a time. At her door, Alice turned to Marco, the warmth in his eyes stirring something deep within her.

"Thank you, Marco," she said. "For everything."

"It's what you do for people you care about," he responded simply, his voice low.

Their eyes held for a long moment before they leaned into each other, sharing a soft, lingering kiss, lessening the tension between them even more. With an affectionate squeeze of her hand, he whispered, "Goodnight, Alice."

"Goodnight," she echoed, watching him retreat down the hallway until he disappeared around the corner.

Closing the door behind her, Alice leaned against it for a moment, a smile tugging at the corners of her lips. The room felt warmer than it had before, and not just because she had escaped the cold. With a contented sigh, she moved away from the door, ready to surrender to the comfort of her bed and the promise of dreams colored by the taste of herbs and the touch of a kiss.

CHAPTER TWENTY THREE

The sun had barely crested the horizon when the incessant shrill of the telephone pierced the morning calm at the château. Alice, already up and trying to figure out what she could do in the garden with her ankle still swollen and painful, felt a twinge of unease as she watched Lilou rush to answer the call, her slippers scuffing against the stone floor in haste.

"Oui, Château DuPont," Lilou's voice echoed through the hallway, tinged with concern. "Quoi? The soil, you say? Salt?"

Alice set her papers aside, her intuition signaling that the trouble which had begun with the hydrangeas was far from over. As calls poured in, one after another, a pattern emerged—a sinister thread weaving through the local vineyards. Each frantic vintner shared the same tale of woe: their precious soil had been sabotaged, just like the earth cradling the hydrangeas. Something had turned spiked the soil with salt and ammonium nitrate fertilizers that could well ruin their crops for the next year or two. As near as anyone could tell, their irrigation systems had been tampered with, delivering poison to their plants as they sought to nourish them with water.

With the phone still clamoring for attention, Alice limped out to seek out Sophie, using a cane Lilou had found for her to keep some weight off her ankle while it healed. She found Sophie standing outside, scrutinizing a cluster of grapevines with the critical eye of a master at work.

"Has our vineyard been tampered with too?" Alice asked, her gaze meeting Sophie's.

Sophie shook her head, a tense look on her face. "No, at least not that I can find. It's only the garden around the château. None of the actual vines."

"Thank goodness for small mercies," Alice murmured, though the furrow between her brows deepened.

"Very lucky," Sophie replied. "Such a relief."

It struck Alice then, the weight of what was at stake—the entire region's wine production could falter for years. It seemed too convenient, too lucky that only the gardens suffered while the vines remained untouched here. Would Château DuPont be the only winery in the area producing rosé for the next few years? And what would all that mean for the rosé competition? The DuPont vineyard had seemingly been spared by fortune or design. With a final glance at the verdant rows of vines, Alice followed the path Sophie had taken, determined to unearth the truth hidden beneath this stroke of 'luck.'

Alice adjusted the brim of her sunhat as she watched the mobile bottling truck roll through the gates of the château, its gleaming presence a stark contrast to the rural charm surrounding it. The side of the truck was emblazoned with "Vin en Vogue" in elegant script, and the workers began preparing for the day's task. Today, they would be bottling the rosé, now christened Soleil Mignon. Despite the recent turmoil, life at the vineyard buzzed with productivity.

She wanted to go in and watch the bottling process, but her ankle throbbed and she knew she would most likely be in the way. Instead, she hobbled back to the kitchen to find Marco clearing the last of their breakfast from the table. The sunlight streamed through the kitchen, casting a warm glow on his dark hair and broad shoulders. He caught her gaze and offered a smile, noticing her distraction.

"Thinking about the new vintage?" he asked, gesturing to the bustle outside.

"Partly," Alice admitted, pulling out a chair to sit down. "It's just that... there's a strange balance of good and bad luck around us lately."

Marco brought another chair around so she could prop up her foot. "How so?" He put a throw pillow beneath her foot.

"Being in the vineyard during the storm, the soil sabotage elsewhere—it all feels orchestrated," she confessed. Alice glanced out the window again, where the workers were now unloading crates of glass bottles, their movements precise and practiced. "Someone knew exactly where I'd be and when I'd be there. Someone tampered only with the soil around the hydrangeas at Château DuPont, but with bigger swatches of soil at the other wineries."

"Someone is playing a dangerous and deceitful game," Marco said thoughtfully, watching her closely.

"Exactly," Alice replied, her eyes narrowing slightly. "And it makes you wonder—why was Château DuPont spared except for those hydrangeas? It's almost as if the hydrangeas were a trial run for what's happening to the vines at the other wineries."

Marco stepped back. "I still don't understand why and what it could mean."

"Me, neither." She sighed. "And how does it connect with René's death? I wish I could put my finger on it."

"Maybe a snack would help," Marco said, putting a small bowl of yogurt with strawberries and blueberries scattered on top in front of Alice.

"Is food always your solution?" she laughed.

He shrugged. "Almost always."

Alice took a bite of the yogurt, tangy on her tongue with the berries adding just the right amount of sweetness. "Whoever did this needed to know exactly how to alter soil conditions in a way that would pass unnoticed until too late."

Marco nodded. "And they'd need a grudge against René strong enough to lead to murder."

"Exactly." She turned to face him, her auburn hair catching the light of the morning sun. "They'd also have to be aware that I wanted to connect with Henri Rousseau to see if he could be involved."

"Who did you tell you were contacting Rousseau?" Marco asked.

Alice swirled her spoon through the yogurt. "I didn't contact him. Sophie contacted him for me, and then he texted me."

"Or we think he texted you," Marco reminded her.

Alice's eyes went wide as she realized the implications of what they'd just said. Sophie would know how to alter soil. Sophie could have lured Alice into the vineyard the night before by texting here from some other phone. She'd been out in the rain, too. They'd all simply taken her word for the fact that she'd been out in the vineyards checking the drains. She could easily have been at Rousseau's slashing Alice's tires.

"Which leads us to Sophie," Marco concluded, reading the suspicion etched into Alice's features.

"Right. Sophie." Alice's voice held a note of reluctance. It pained her to suspect another woman who shared her love for the land and all it could be. She'd felt such a connection with her. "But why? She praised René, said he taught her everything she knows."

"Then why would she want him dead?" Marco asked, pushing off the counter to sit down across from Alice at the table.

"Because perhaps that praise was only a performance." Alice stopped again, her gaze drifting toward the windows and out into the gardens with the vineyards beyond. "As I've poked around, I've heard nothing but comments about how René might not have been the master vintner he wanted everyone to believe him to be. Claire LeBlanc didn't think much of his winemaking skills. Geoffrey Lambert didn't think much of his palate. Lucille Girard didn't respect his knowledge of plants. Jean-Baptiste mentioned that he'd meddle in things and make problems, sometimes at the last minute when they couldn't be undone. He'd done the same to you years ago. Perhaps he was going to do something to the rosé. Sophie told me how much it meant to her and how much it might mean to her career. She'd want to protect it."

Marco raised an eyebrow, interest piqued. "You think Sophie was the real talent behind the wine?"

"Yes. René had a reputation for being a bit... scattered. Some say he ruined more batches than he perfected." A shadow of doubt crossed Alice's face as she considered the woman she had come to admire. It was a troubling thought, but the pieces were aligning like rows of grapevines pointing to the truth. "Sophie could have been doing all the work while René soaked up the accolades."

"If she also knew about the potential deal between René and Claire LeBlanc, she might have worried that she was about to be pushed out of a job, too. Claire would be more than capable of taking over the winemaking here," Marco said.

"So she'd be out of a job and not able to capitalize on all her successes. If Sophie had the freedom to implement her own vision," Alice said, waving her spoon at Marco, "she wouldn't have to be constantly on the lookout for René meddling and potentially ruining the wine."

"Pure autonomy," Marco agreed, leaning back in his chair. "She could innovate without restraint, get the recognition she believes she deserves."

"Exactly," Alice confirmed with a swift nod. "No more ghostwriting the story of this vineyard. She becomes the author and the protagonist."

Marco furrowed his brow, the morning light catching in the tousled waves of his dark hair. "But how can we prove that enough for it to be motive? Accolades are one thing, but murder..."

Alice met his gaze, her own filled with a resolve sharpened by the morning's discoveries. "We need to tread carefully, Marco. This vineyard has already seen too much turmoil. We could be wrong."

"What do you suggest?" he asked.

"I'm not entirely sure yet," she admitted. "But I have an idea."

Reaching for her phone, she scrolled through her contacts until she found the number she was looking for. Her thumb hesitated for just a moment before she pressed 'call'. The line clicked, and she spoke with a clarity that belied her racing heart. "Inspector Fournier? It's Alice Bloom at Château DuPont. I've found something that might interest you. Could you come over?"

"Something related to René Dupont's case?" The inspector's voice carried the weariness of countless cases, yet a thread of intrigue.

"Potentially," Alice replied, her words carefully chosen. "It's about the vineyard... and what's beneath it."

"Very well," he said after a pause. "I'll be there within the hour."

"Thank you," she said, ending the call. She looked up to find Marco watching her, his expression a blend of admiration and worry.

"Let's hope whatever you've got brewing in that mind of yours leads us to some answers," he said, his voice steady despite the uncertainty that hung between them like the fragile tendrils of a new vine reaching for support.

"Yes, Marco," Alice murmured, her resolve fortified. "For René's sake, and for the château's future."

CHAPTER TWENTY FOUR

Alice's ankle protested with each step, but the pull of curiosity was stronger than the dull ache. The scent of fermenting grapes led her to the winery where Sophie, with sleeves rolled up and hair tied back, was checking the stainless-steel vats . Alice leaned against the cool entrance doorframe, watching.

"Can I watch?" Alice asked, her voice echoing slightly in the cavernous space filled with the symphony of bottling machinery whirring into action. "I don't want to be in the way."

Sophie glanced over her shoulder, her face brightening. "Come in," she said, waving Alice in and pointing to a chair. "Just in time for the final act."

Sophie withdrew a sample of the rosé from a vat with a thief, the clear tube returning with its colorful prisoner. She swirled the liquid in a wine glass, examining it against the light that spilled through the high windows.

"Perfect clarity," Sophie murmured, more to herself than to Alice.

Her lips met the edge of the glass, and she took a delicate sip, eyes closing in concentration. After a moment of thoughtful silence, she nodded in approval and poured another glass for Alice.

"Try this," Sophie said, extending the stemware with a flourish. "Tell me what you think."

Alice accepted the glass. She admired the rosé's hue, reminiscent of a gentle sunset captured within the curve of the glass. The name was apt. Pretty sun. Taking a sip, the flavors of summer berries and a hint of floral notes played across her palate, balanced with a crisp acidity that made her tastebuds sing.

"I liked it before," Alice admitted, placing the glass down with care, "but this... this is something else. It's exceptional."

A shadow of pride flickered across Sophie's face, her eyes reflecting the depth of the wine before her. "Thank you, Alice," she replied. "That means a lot coming from someone with your taste."

The two women shared a smile, the air around them rich with the promise of the upcoming harvest and the subtle notes of victory hidden within the depths of the ruby liquid. Alice hoped she was wrong. She liked this woman. Respected and admired her. *Please don't let her be a murderer.*

Sophie's adjusted the gleaming steel knobs on the bottling machine. The hum of the mechanism filled the space.

"René never wanted these adjustments," Sophie confided over the mechanical buzz, casting a glance at the rows of empty bottles waiting like silent sentinels. "But I knew they'd elevate the rosé. It was the right thing to do."

Alice followed Sophie's gaze, the question forming in her mind as naturally as dew on morning petals. "What if you get to stay on at DuPont? With the news about the tainted soil at other vineyards, what then?"

The corner of Sophie's mouth curled into a small smile. "Then, I suppose I'll keep winning competition after competition." Her eyes held a glint.

Taking a deep breath and then letting out slowly, she asked what she really wanted to know, "Is that why you killed René?" The words dropped like overripe fruit from a branch. "So he wouldn't meddle with the wine and you could win the competition and finally be recognized for your work?"

Sophie's expression faltered for only a fraction of a second before she regained her composure, her smile tightening. "Kill René?" She feigned confusion, turning back to the bottles. "I'm not sure what you're talking about, Alice. I thought you'd decided he'd poisoned himself with hemlock from his own garden."

The steady rhythm of the machinery punctuated the moment. Alice leaned in. "I understand why you did it, Sophie," she said, her voice low and steady. The hum of machinery seemed to pause as if eavesdropping on their clandestine exchange.

Sophie's hands, stilled on the stainless-steel table. Her eyes darted away, then back, searching Alice's face.

"Owen takes all the credit for my designs," Alice continued, her own hands fiddling with the wineglass stem. The rosé within swirled, casting a delicate dance of light. "Everyone thinks it's his vision I'm executing, that I'm just a technician."

In her mind, Alice mentally apologized to Owen, acknowledging his gruff yet unwavering support. He grumbled, sure, but he fostered her growth like a gardener tends a rare bloom and always praised her in public and private. She needed to bond with Sophie, though, and how better to do it than over shared injustices, real or imagined.

"Working so hard on something beautiful, only to have someone swoop in at the last minute..." Alice shook her head, allowing a hint of frustration to color her tone. "They either ruin everything you've done, or they take all the glory. And if things go wrong? You're the one left holding the spade."

Sophie's posture relaxed. "Exactly," she whispered, almost to herself. "You do understand."

Alice set down her glass, the liquid's hue a perfect echo of the twilight sky outside. "René was going to muck up the rosé you'd perfected," she said, a note of empathy threading through her words. "But René could only fool so many people. Word was getting around that you were the real brains behind this new rosé. This competition must have felt like your chance to escape from under his shadow."

The corners of Sophie's lips twitched, not quite forming a smile, but the relief in her gaze was palpable. She looked at the rows of bottles aligned with military precision, each one a vessel for her silenced dreams and aspirations. With René out of the picture, those dreams had found their voice.

"Sometimes, you just have to prune away the deadwood," Alice added softly, her eyes never leaving Sophie's face.

"Sometimes, you do," Sophie echoed, a quiet determination settling over her features like dusk upon the vineyard rows.

Alice leaned in, her keen eyes catching the subtle shift in Sophie's stance, the way her hands trembled ever so slightly as they rested on the cool stainless steel of the wine vat. "You've tended to this vineyard with the same care I give my gardens," Alice said, her voice a gentle murmur. "It's more than just work. It's even more than art. It's our hearts and our souls."

Sophie's eyes widened, their deep brown hue reflecting a storm of emotions. "I... I didn't think anyone would understand," she confessed, her shoulders dropping as if unburdened by an invisible weight. "But speaking to you now, it feels like a breath of fresh air after being stifled for so long." She glanced around the winery, its walls lined with oak barrels that bore the silent witness to her strife. "René— he was like a blight on healthy vines. Every time I tried to cultivate something beautiful, he'd come along and tarnish it with his touch."

Alice listened, the winery's faintly sweet aroma mingling with a growing tension in the air. She noted the earnestness in Sophie's expression, the way her confession seemed to sprout from a hidden seed of desperation.

"René was going to ruin everything," Sophie continued, her voice barely rising above the hum of the cooling system. "The rosé... my rosé... he couldn't see what it could become. He was an idiot who ruined everything he touched. Then I found out he was going to merge Château DuPont with Château LeBlanc and put Claire in charge of winemaking. The two of them would meet late in the evening when René was on one of his walks. I overheard them talking when I was out checking the vines one night. This competition would be my last and only moment to make my reputation."

"So you poisoned him?" Alice asked.

Sophie nodded. "Yes. I brought him a cup of tea that night when he was out in the garden. Everyone was used to me making tea before bed. No one watched. It was easy enough to slip a preparation of hemlock that I'd made in the lab into the cup. He drank every drop."

There was a silence then, filled only by the distant sound of corks being sorted for bottling.

"And Alice," Sophie added, her voice softening, "I need to apologize to you." Her fingers gripped the edge of the table, knuckles whitening. "That night, during the storm..." She paused, taking a shaky breath. "I never wanted to harm you. It was foolish, but I thought if I could just frighten you, you'd stop looking into things. Stop getting close to the truth. You were eliminating suspects left and right and I couldn't assume Fournier was stupid enough to keep focusing his investigation on you and Marco."

Alice held her gaze steady, processing the confession with the same careful consideration she'd give to diagnosing a mysterious plant ailment. "I appreciate your honesty, Sophie," she said, her tone remaining even though her mind raced with the implications of Sophie's words. "But scaring me wasn't the way to deal with this."

"I know, I know," Sophie admitted, the clatter of a rolling wine bottle punctuating her remorse. "I was desperate. You have to understand, I needed to protect what I've worked for... what I've built here."

"Desperation can lead us down paths we never thought we'd take," Alice replied, her own experience with stubborn weeds and unruly vines lending her a sense of empathy. "And sometimes, those paths have thorns we don't see until it's too late."

Sophie nodded, a rueful smile tugging at the corner of her mouth, as if recognizing a kindred spirit in the landscape artist before her. "Thank you, Alice," she said quietly. "For listening and understanding."

"Of course," Alice responded, yet within her, alarm bells rang—a symphony of cautionary tones that reminded her that understanding was not the same as absolution.

The clink of the wine bottle rolling to a stop was suddenly drowned out by the creak of the winery door opening. Both women turned towards the sound, their conversation about poisonous intentions interrupted by the imposing silhouette of Inspector Fournier framed in the doorway. His shadow stretched across the stone floor like an accusation, cool and long in the afternoon sun.

"Mademoiselle Moreau," he announced with a voice that seemed to echo off the fermentation tanks, "I am placing you under arrest for the murder of René Dupont."

Sophie's face drained of color, her hands trembling slightly as they left the reassurance of the glass she had been holding.

"Inspector, I—" Sophie began, but Fournier held up a hand.

"Please, spare me the theatrics," he said crisply. "I've heard quite enough."

He moved into the room with the confidence of someone who had all the pieces of the puzzle neatly arranged. The clasp of the handcuffs glinted in the light as he approached, the metallic sound incongruous in the serene space where grapes were transformed into award-winning wines.

Alice watched, her heart thudding in her chest like the beat of nature's own rhythm.

"Inspector Fournier, you were listening?" Sophie's voice was barely a whisper, a leaf quivering on the verge of falling.

"Indeed," he confirmed, securing the cuffs around her wrists. "From the moment I suspected your guilt, I found it prudent to keep an ear close to the ground. It seems my instincts were correct."

Alice only barely kept herself from rolling her eyes. He'd never suspected Sophie. He'd been too busy suspecting her and Marco. At least, he came through at the end. She supposed that was something. Fournier was more like René DuPont than he'd want to admit.

Sophie hung her head, her defiance seeping away into the soil of her misdeeds. Alice couldn't help but feel a pang of compassion for the woman who had let ambition cloud her judgment and sow seeds of destruction.

Just as Fournier began to lead Sophie away, Alice remembered one last loose thread she hadn't been able to weave in. "Sophie! Was it you that poisoned the soil around the hydrangeas?"

"Of course, you'd be concerned about the plants." Sophie stopped and shook her head. "Look. For some reason, René loved those hydrangeas. He said it was because his mother loved them, but every photo I've seen of her has her with the roses. It seemed fitting to destroy them the way he was destroying my dreams. I experimented on them to find ways to ruin other people's crops. I added ammonium nitrate, but the only thing that happened was a color change. I needed more. I wanted to take out all of my competition. That's when I turned to salt. That worked like a dream."

"More like a nightmare," Alice said.

As Sophie was led away, the winery fell quiet. Then Marco came in, putting an arm around Alice. "You did it. You were right. She wanted someone to understand, and you gave her that."

Alice turned into his hug. "I feel sorry for her. She should have been able to get what she wanted without resorting to murder. To be recognized for your work is not so much to ask."

EPILOGUE

Alice pressed the last paver into place, her hands firm and steady despite the ache in her muscles. She wiped a bead of sweat from her brow, her hair sticking to the side of her face. She stood slowly, being careful about how much weight she put on her ankle. Standing back, she admired the newly installed patio—a modest tribute to René—with its neat, interlocking stones and the centerpiece: a wrought iron bench adorned with a small, engraved plaque that read "In Memory of René Dupont." It was oriented to look out at the vine-covered hills.

She hesitated for a moment before planting herself on the bench. The garden was different now. It still had the vintage roses that had been here when she arrived. She'd kept the lavender that had been here, too. The yew was gone and beds were filled with herbs and flowers that all could be used in the kitchen. Alice had poured her soul into every leaf and petal.

"Looks like you've outdone yourself once again, Alice." Marco's voice broke the silence, and she turned to find him approaching with an appreciative smile.

"Thank you, Marco," she said, rising to meet him. "It felt right to honor René's memory in this way. He wasn't perfect, but he loved these gardens and wanted them to flourish."

Marco's dark hair ruffled slightly in the breeze. "He would have been proud," Marco said. "And speaking of pride, I'm proud to know someone as talented and passionate as you."

"Flattery will get you everywhere," Alice teased, her spirits lifted by his presence.

"Good to know," Marco chuckled. "But honestly, I've been thinking..."

"About?" Alice arched an eyebrow in curiosity, her heart rate subtly quickening.

"Us." He reached out, taking her hand gently in his broad one. "We both travel so much, and it seems we only see each other by sheer luck."

"True," Alice conceded, feeling the warmth of his touch seep through her. "So, what do you propose?"

"Let's not leave it to chance anymore." Marco's gaze held hers with an intensity that made the world around them fade. "Let's make plans, actual plans to see each other. Could be here, could be anywhere you're designing your next masterpiece."

"Intentional meetings?" Alice mused, the idea both thrilling and comforting. "I think I'd like that. It's... nice to have something to look forward to."

"Exactly," he said, squeezing her hand. "And besides, who else is going to taste-test my latest batch of edible flowers?"

"Or give you unsolicited advice on sustainable landscaping?" she added with a playful smirk.

"Wouldn't want it any other way," Marco replied, his laughter mingling with hers, as natural and easy as the wind rustling through the leaves.

"Then it's a date," Alice said, her words sealing their new promise as they stood together, surrounded by the beauty of a garden that whispered tales of life, legacy, and new beginnings.

The car made its way up the drive with Jean-Baptiste at the wheel. He got out and opened the door for a young woman. René's daughter, Gabrielle DuPont, with her easy stride and an air of decision about her, joined Alice and Marco by the newly laid patio.

She'd arrived a few days ago and was quickly figuring out what she wanted to do with her family's winery.

"Hello, you two," she greeted them. "I hope I'm not interrupting."

"Of course not, Gabrielle," Alice replied, noticing the subtle shift in Marco's stance—a protective, almost brotherly aura taking shape. "What brings you out here?"

Gabrielle exhaled, her gaze sweeping across the hydrangeas and resting on the bench bearing her father's name. "I've pulled our wine out of the rosé competition," she said with a sad smile. "And I wanted to tell you both that Soleil Mignon isn't going anywhere. We're not selling it."

Alice's eyes widened slightly at the news. "But the competition is such a highlight for the region," she remarked, her voice tinged with genuine disappointment. "And it is a lovely wine . . ."

"A lovely wine made by a murderer." Gabrielle put her hands on her hips and turned in a slow circle. "This however, what you've made here, Alice. This will remain."

"I'm so glad," Alice said. "So, have you made a decision about what will happen to Château DuPont?"

Gabrielle sat down next to her on the bench. "I've gone forward with Dad's plans to merge with Claire LeBlanc. The feud between our families was ridiculous. I'll need Claire's winemaking expertise to keep going. Lilou has agreed to stay on as facilities manager. Jean-Baptiste will be staying on as well."

"And you, Gabrielle? Will you stay on?" Marco asked.

She smiled a small smile. "I think I just might. There's something about this place, about the light and the air and the soil."

Alice smiled up at Marco. "It's magical."

"It is," Gabrielle agreed.

"Hold on just a moment," Marco said. "I'll be right back."

Alice and Gabrielle sat in contented silence, looking out over the family estate. Marco returned a bottle of sparkling wine, three glasses, and a plate gougères. "The wine was sent over by Claire LeBlanc and Lilou taught me to make the gougères this morning. I think the combination might be the perfect thing to toast this new beginning."

He poured glasses for all three of them.

"Here's to new beginnings," Alice said, lifting her glass to catch the light, its contents shimmering like the morning dew.

"To remembering the past," Marco added, his voice steady and sincere.

"And to protecting what matters," Gabrielle concluded, the corners of her eyes crinkling with a smile.

Their glasses clinked, a delicate symphony to accompany the birdsong and whispers of the garden. Alice sipped the wine, its flavor complex and comforting, much like the journey that had led them all here.

NOW AVAILABLE!

A MYSTERY IN BLOOM: DECEIT IN THE DAFFODILS
(An Alice Bloom Cozy Mystery—Book 3)

On the idyllic isles of Greece, landscape designer Alice Bloom crafts a labyrinthine garden that becomes an unexpected crime scene when her client, a reclusive artist, meets an untimely demise.

As romance intertwines with mystery under Mediterranean skies, can Alice's botanical expertise unveil the murderer before another victim is claimed?

A Mystery in Bloom: Deceit in the Daffodils (An Alice Bloom Cozy Mystery—Book 3) is the third novel in a new series by cozy mystery author Fiona Grace. The series begins with A Mystery in Bloom: Murder in the Marigolds (Book 1).

The Alice Bloom series is a page-turning, charming cozy mystery that invites you into a picturesque setting, packed with humor, romance, and surprise twists and turns. You'll be up well past bedtime as you fall in love with your new favorite female protagonist.

Future books in the series are also available!

Fiona Grace

Fiona Grace is author of the LACEY DOYLE COZY MYSTERY series, comprising nine books; of the TUSCAN VINEYARD COZY MYSTERY series, comprising seven books; of the DUBIOUS WITCH COZY MYSTERY series, comprising three books; of the BEACHFRONT BAKERY COZY MYSTERY series, comprising six books; of the CATS AND DOGS COZY MYSTERY series, comprising nine books; of the ELIZA MONTAGU COZY MYSTERY series, comprising nine books (and counting); of the ENDLESS HARBOR ROMANTIC COMEDY series, comprising nine books (and counting); of the INN AT DUNE ISLAND ROMANTIC COMEDY series, comprising five books (and counting); of the INN BY THE SEA ROMANTIC COMEDY series, comprising five books (and counting); of the MAID AND THE MANSION COZY MYSTERY series, comprising five books (and counting); of the ALICE BLOOM COZY MYSTERY series, comprising five books (and counting); and of the TIMBERLAKE TITANS HOCKEY ROMANCE series, comprising five books (and counting).

Fiona would love to hear from you, so please visit www.fionagraceauthor.com to receive free ebooks, hear the latest news, and stay in touch.

BOOKS BY FIONA GRACE

TIMBERLAKE TITANS HOCKEY ROMANCE
RINKSIDE ROMANCE (Book #1)
FLIRTY FACEOFF (Book #2)
MELTING THE ICE (Book #3)
THE PUCK STOPS HERE (Book #4)
GLOVES DROP, LOVE BLOOMS (Book #5)

THE MAID AND THE MANSION COZY MYSTERY
A MYSTERIOUS MURDER (Book #1)
A SCANDALOUS DEATH (Book #2)
A MISSING GUEST (Book #3)
AN UNSOLVABLE CRIME (Book #4)
AN IMPOSSIBLE HEIST (Book #5)

INN BY THE SEA ROMANTIC COMEDY
A NEW LOVE (Book #1)
A NEW CHANCE (Book #2)
A NEW HOME (Book #3)
A NEW LIFE (Book #4)
A NEW ME (Book #5)

THE INN AT DUNE ISLAND ROMANTIC COMEDY
A CHANCE LOVE (Book #1)
A CHANCE FALL (Book #2)
A CHANCE ROMANCE (Book #3)
A CHANCE CHRISTMAS (Book #4)
A CHANCE ENGAGEMENT (Book #5)

ENDLESS HARBOR ROMANTIC COMEDY
ALWAYS, WITH YOU (Book #1)
ALWAYS, FOREVER (Book #2)
ALWAYS, PLUS ONE (Book #3)
ALWAYS, TOGETHER (Book #4)
ALWAYS, LIKE THIS (Book #5)
ALWAYS, FATED (Book #6)
ALWAYS, FOR LOVE (Book #7)
ALWAYS, JUST US (Book #8)

ALWAYS, IN LOVE (Book #9)

ELIZA MONTAGU COZY MYSTERY
MURDER AT THE HEDGEROW (Book #1)
A DALLOP OF DEATH (Book #2)
CALAMITY AT THE BALL (Book #3)
A SPEAKEASY DEMISE (Book #4)
A FLAPPER FATALITY (Book #5)
BUMPED BY A DAME (Book #6)
A DOLL'S DEBACLE (Book #7)
A FELLA'S RUIN (Book #8)
A GAL'S OFFING (Book #9)

LACEY DOYLE COZY MYSTERY
MURDER IN THE MANOR (Book#1)
DEATH AND A DOG (Book #2)
CRIME IN THE CAFE (Book #3)
VEXED ON A VISIT (Book #4)
KILLED WITH A KISS (Book #5)
PERISHED BY A PAINTING (Book #6)
SILENCED BY A SPELL (Book #7)
FRAMED BY A FORGERY (Book #8)
CATASTROPHE IN A CLOISTER (Book #9)

TUSCAN VINEYARD COZY MYSTERY
AGED FOR MURDER (Book #1)
AGED FOR DEATH (Book #2)
AGED FOR MAYHEM (Book #3)
AGED FOR SEDUCTION (Book #4)
AGED FOR VENGEANCE (Book #5)
AGED FOR ACRIMONY (Book #6)
AGED FOR MALICE (Book #7)

DUBIOUS WITCH COZY MYSTERY
SKEPTIC IN SALEM: AN EPISODE OF MURDER (Book #1)
SKEPTIC IN SALEM: AN EPISODE OF CRIME (Book #2)
SKEPTIC IN SALEM: AN EPISODE OF DEATH (Book #3)

BEACHFRONT BAKERY COZY MYSTERY
BEACHFRONT BAKERY: A KILLER CUPCAKE (Book #1)
BEACHFRONT BAKERY: A MURDEROUS MACARON (Book #2)

BEACHFRONT BAKERY: A PERILOUS CAKE POP (Book #3)
BEACHFRONT BAKERY: A DEADLY DANISH (Book #4)
BEACHFRONT BAKERY: A TREACHEROUS TART (Book #5)
BEACHFRONT BAKERY: A CALAMITOUS COOKIE (Book #6)

CATS AND DOGS COZY MYSTERY
A VILLA IN SICILY: OLIVE OIL AND MURDER (Book #1)
A VILLA IN SICILY: FIGS AND A CADAVER (Book #2)
A VILLA IN SICILY: VINO AND DEATH (Book #3)
A VILLA IN SICILY: CAPERS AND CALAMITY (Book #4)
A VILLA IN SICILY: ORANGE GROVES AND VENGEANCE (Book #5)
A VILLA IN SICILY: CANNOLI AND A CASUALTY (Book #6)

ALICE BLOOM COZY MYSTERY
MURDER IN THE MARIGOLDS (Book #1)
RUIN IN THE ROSES (Book #2)
DECEIT IN THE DAFFODILS (Book #3)
SCANDAL IN THE SAFFRON (Book #4)
CATASTROPHE IN THE CARNATIONS (Book #5)

Made in United States
North Haven, CT
13 July 2024

54729525R00093